replica

Lucky Thirteen

MARILYN KAYE

BANTAM BOOKS
NEW YORK • TORONTO • LONDON • SYDNEY • AUCKLAND

RL 5.5, 008–012
LUCKY THIRTEEN
A Bantam Skylark Book / April 2000

For information address: Bantam Books.

ISBN 0-553-48712-4

Published simultaneously in the United States and Canada

Bantam Skylark is an imprint of Random House Children's Books, a division of Random House, Inc. SKYLARK BOOK, BANTAM BOOKS, and the rooster colophon are registered trademarks of Random House, Inc.

PRINTED IN THE UNITED STATES OF AMERICA

OPM 10 9 8 7 6 5 4 3 2 1

For the Garretts—Liz, Hugh,
Guinn, and Annie

Lucky Thirteen

one

"Okay, we've done the roller coaster, the space commando thing, and the bumper cars," Eric announced. "What's next?"

"How about the Ferris wheel?" Amy suggested. "Or we could try a game. What do you want to do, Tasha?"

"Whatever," Tasha replied. She was too busy looking around the carnival grounds in search of something or someone to care what they did. Amy shrugged. She didn't care either. She was happy just to walk around and take in all the sights and sounds.

There was something special about a carnival at night. Bright lights pierced the darkness; the tinkling music of the merry-go-round provided the perfect background for the shrill calls of the carnival workers; the giggles of the people aiming fake rifles at fake ducks were full of contagious fun; the distant shrieks coming from the roller coaster and the top of the Ferris wheel filled the air; and a warm breeze carried the tantalizing aromas of cotton candy and hot buttered popcorn.

"It's funny," Amy mused. "I saw them setting the carnival up this afternoon, and it looked kind of lame. You know, the booths were dirty and run-down, and you could see rust stains on the carousel horses. But at night it's magical! There's a mysterious atmosphere, there's a sense of danger in the air."

Eric didn't agree. "What's mysterious about it? This carnival's no different than it was last year or the year before that. And these rides aren't dangerous. I've been riding them since I was five."

He was right, of course. The traveling carnival materialized in the same open field for the same two weeks every year. There was nothing spectacular about it. The games, the rides, even the food were always the same. Like most southern California kids, Amy had been to Disneyland, and she had to admit that this carnival was no big deal by comparison. The biggest danger lurking in the shadows was maybe a pickpocket, or some obnoxious kid who tried to grab your hard-won stuffed animal.

But even so, Amy loved it. The colors, the smells, and the noises weren't the same ones she saw and smelled and heard every day, so it *was* special. And she wasn't going to let Eric's "been there, done that" attitude ruin it for her.

"Want to get in line for the Ferris wheel?" she asked Tasha.

"Not yet." Tasha's eyes searched the crowd again. "Do you see him?"

"Who?"

"I *told* you. Dwayne said he'd be here tonight. Remember?"

Amy remembered. She just preferred to forget. "I can't believe you're into Dwayne Hicks."

"Why not? Don't you think he's cute?"

Amy couldn't deny that. Their classmate bore a remarkable resemblance to Leonardo DiCaprio. But in Amy's opinion, being a Leo look-alike was just about all Dwayne had going for him. "He's cute," she acknowledged. "But that's it."

"Oh, come on," Tasha protested. "Can't you think of anything nice to say about him?"

Amy considered the question. "Well, he's not a psychotic serial killer."

Tasha sighed. "What do you have against Dwayne?"

"Nothing," Amy replied. "But he's not exactly a mental giant."

"Brains aren't everything," Tasha shot back.

"I just think you can do a lot better."

Tasha made a face. "That's easy for you to say."

Tasha had a point. Amy and Tasha's older brother, Eric, had been together for a while now, so Amy wasn't looking for a boyfriend. Personally, Amy didn't believe it was absolutely essential to have a boyfriend—she and Eric had just sort of come together naturally.

But at that moment, in the seventh grade at Parkside Middle School, all the girls were talking about boyfriends, real or potential. Tasha wanted one too. And she'd set her sights on Dwayne.

"Are you *sure* you can't see him?" Tasha pressed. "Are you even *trying*?"

Amy knew what Tasha was referring to. She wanted Amy to use her special vision, her unique ability to see farther and more distinctly, even in the dark, than regular human beings.

Amy complied. Concentrating, she surveyed the scene. She identified a couple of girls from school on a ride, and she saw her math teacher trying to fish a prize out of a gigantic bowl. But there was no sign of Dwayne.

"I could probably spot him from the top of the Ferris wheel," she proposed, but Tasha shook her head.

"I want to wait and go on that with Dwayne," she confessed. Amy didn't need superior vision to see that her best friend was blushing. Amy glanced at Eric, but he was doing the guy thing and ignoring his sister.

Then Tasha grabbed Amy's arm, and Amy assumed this meant she'd spotted Dwayne. But she was wrong. "Ooh, look, there's the fortune-teller's tent. Let's go over!"

The proposition didn't thrill Amy, but at least it might take her friend's mind off Dwayne for a while. "Okay," she agreed. "Eric, how about getting your palm read?"

"No thanks," he replied.

"Oh, come on," Amy wheedled. "Don't you want to know your future?"

"I already know my future," Eric said. "I'm gonna flunk Spanish."

"That's a gloomy prediction," Amy said, laughing.

"Tell me about it. We've got an unbelievable assignment," he told her. "We have to translate this entire Spanish *book* by next week." He amended that. "Okay, it's not a book, but it's a really long story. And I'm stuck on the verbs."

"Can't you get some extra help?" Amy asked him. "Like a tutor?"

"I'm working on it." He looked at her hopefully. "Are you offering your services?"

"I'm taking French, not Spanish," she reminded him.

"I know, but you could learn the entire Spanish language in an hour," he pointed out.

That was an exaggeration but not too far from the truth. Amy's extraordinary skills included the ability to learn just about anything in much less time than it took normal people. But it bothered her that Eric always took it for granted that she would use her abilities to help him out at school. "Sorry, but I don't want to learn Spanish. Not now, anyway."

"Gee, what's the point of having a genetically engineered girlfriend if I can't take advantage of her genius IQ?"

"Oh, shut up," Amy said. She knew he was just teasing, but comments like that got on her nerves. "And keep your voice down, okay?"

"You can't have it both ways," Eric said cheerfully. "I can either shut up or keep my voice down." Clearly, he wasn't particularly upset by Amy's unwillingness to help him out. But she did wish he would remember that his voice had a tendency to carry.

Not that anyone would believe anything they'd overheard. Strolling across the carnival grounds with her friends, Amy knew she looked like an ordinary twelve-year-old girl. With her average height and weight, her straight brown hair, her brown eyes, there was nothing amazing or unusual about her appearance. No one could tell that she had been created in a laboratory. No one could even come close to guessing that she had been cloned from carefully selected genetic material. That her designed DNA made her the most intelligent, the most athletic, the most gifted twelve-year-old girl around. And that somewhere in the world there were eleven others exactly like her.

They'd reached the fortune-teller's tent, which was decorated with glittering stars and astrological signs. A sign hanging on the front flaps indicated that the tent was currently occupied. "Someone's in there," Amy pointed out to Tasha. "We can come back later." Or never, she added silently.

"We'll wait," Tasha said firmly. "I've got to get some questions answered."

"I'll be over at the ring toss," Eric told them, and sauntered away.

Fortunately, they didn't have to wait too long. A girl came out of the tent smiling a very happy smile. "She looks like she got her money's worth," Tasha whispered.

"Of course she did," Amy replied. "These fortune-tellers always tell you what you want to hear. It's such a scam, Tasha. First they tell you a little something just to get you curious, then they tell you they need more money if you want to know anything else."

But Tasha wasn't put off. She was gazing expectantly at the woman who had followed the girl out of the tent. In her turquoise pantsuit, with her gray hair gathered in a bun and little laugh lines around her eyes, the woman looked more like someone's grandmother than the stereotype of a Gypsy fortune-teller. The woman beamed at them.

"Palms or cards?" she asked.

It was then that Amy noticed the sign by the tent: Tarot card readings cost ten dollars, palm readings five. "Can you take us both together?" she asked hopefully. "Two palms for the price of one?"

Tasha glared at her. "Don't be ridiculous. I'll go first," she declared, and the woman ushered her in.

Left on her own, Amy wandered over to a nearby refreshment tent and bought a candy apple. Licking the sticky-sweet shell, she gazed around to see if anyone she knew was strolling past. Lots of young teens were wandering around on this first night of the carnival, but there were plenty of middle schools in Los Angeles. She didn't see anyone from Parkside.

She didn't see her mother, either. Nancy Candler was at the carnival with Dr. David Hopkins, but Amy didn't want to run into them. It wasn't that she didn't like Dr. Hopkins—she was actually very fond of him—but she was hoping a romantic relationship would develop between the two old friends, and her tagging along wouldn't help.

Amy contemplated the possibility of Dr. Hopkins's becoming her stepfather. It wasn't an unpleasant notion. Since she'd never had a father, it wasn't like he'd be taking anyone's place. And having a husband just might shift Nancy's mind off Amy once in a while.

To be fair, Amy knew it couldn't be easy for Nancy to have a daughter like her. Some parents considered themselves blessed to have an unusually gifted child, but they didn't usually encounter sinister people who wanted to snatch their child away. Nancy had, and it gave her plenty to worry about. The same was true for Amy.

Both Nancy Candler and David Hopkins had been scientists with Project Crescent back in Washington, D.C., just over twelve years ago. The project members thought the purpose of their experiments in cloning was to find cures for genetic disorders. But Dr. James Jaleski, the director of the project, had discovered the terrible truth: The organization that had funded the top-secret government project intended to use the genetically perfect clones to create a master race.

So the scientists decided to terminate the project and destroy all the evidence. The twelve female infant clones—Amy, Number One, through Amy, Number Twelve—were sent to adoption agencies all over the world. At the same time, the scientists planted a bomb to demolish the laboratory. They hoped the organization would think the clones had died in the explosion.

Nancy Candler had taken Amy, Number Seven, to raise as her own daughter. It wasn't until recently, when Amy became aware of her unusual skills, that she had found out the truth about herself. At that point she and her mother realized that others might also suspect the truth—that the clones had not been destroyed. That the clones were still out there somewhere, alive and well, and that the creation of a master race was still a possibility.

Just thinking about it made Amy's skin crawl. Tossing the stick and the core of the candy apple into a trash can, she went back to the fortune-teller's tent to wait for Tasha.

Tasha emerged from her session looking enthralled. "Amy, this fortune-teller is amazing!"

"Cool," Amy said agreeably, trying to hide her skepticism. She followed the woman into the tent.

"Do you want a tarot reading or a palm reading?" the woman asked, sitting at a little table.

Amy recalled which had been cheaper. "Palm," she said promptly, and took a seat facing the woman. She extended her hand and the fortune-teller took it, staring at Amy's palm intently.

The woman's brow furrowed. "You're very unusual," she said. "You're not like most girls. But you are not alone. There are others."

Someone more gullible might have thought the fortune-teller was right on target. But Amy wasn't about to fall for her dramatic pronouncement. Her words could be interpreted many ways, to fit anyone's ideas about herself. That was how these people operated.

"That's true," Amy said, just to be polite.

The woman continued to study her palm. "This is a tough one," she murmured. "It's not easy to read. Hmmm."

Amy wasn't impressed. She was sure the fortune-teller said that to everyone. Most people wanted to think that their palms were more interesting than other people's.

"You will meet a stranger."

Amy couldn't resist rolling her eyes at this tired old line. "You mean a mysterious stranger?" she asked. "Tall, dark, and handsome?"

The fortune-teller ignored her sarcasm. "No . . . not mysterious. You will recognize this stranger."

"If I can recognize this stranger, then he or she can't be a stranger," Amy pointed out.

The woman's eyes didn't leave her palm. Her grip on Amy's wrist tightened. "A stranger," she said again, "a stranger whom you will know. And this stranger will be very important to you."

"Because we'll fall madly in love and he'll carry me away to his desert island, where we'll live happily ever after?"

"This stranger can change your life."

"For better or worse?" Amy joked.

The woman looked into Amy's eyes. "Don't laugh, young lady. And you must be very, very careful. Because this stranger may be your best friend. Or your worst enemy."

Amy squirmed in her seat. The woman's gaze was unsettling, and she didn't look like a jolly grandmother anymore. Her eyes had gone dark.

With some force, Amy jerked her hand away. "That's enough. I don't believe in this stuff anyway."

To her surprise, the fortune-teller didn't urge her to stay. "I understand. Maybe it's better for you not to know too much."

This was getting creepy. Amy had a sudden urge to get out of the tent as fast as possible. "I have to go now," she said abruptly. She got up and left.

Tasha was surprised to see her back so soon. "You're finished already?"

Amy shook off the uneasy feelings. "It's all so stupid. You don't really buy into this, do you?" It dawned on her that she hadn't paid the fortune-teller. But the woman didn't come running after her, and Amy had no desire to seek her out again.

"I'm not really sure," Tasha said thoughtfully. "A lot of intelligent people believe in psychics, you know. There's even scientific evidence that some folks have the gift of seeing into the future."

"What did she tell *you*?" Amy asked.

Tasha smiled happily. "She said that a certain boy right here at the carnival is thinking about me and wondering where I am."

Amy nodded. "I believe that."

"You do?"

"Sure. Aren't we supposed to meet Eric at the ring toss? He's probably wondering where we are right now."

Tasha stuck out her tongue. "Very funny. I'm *sure* she was talking about Dwayne. You know, you could help me find him if you tried."

Amy groaned. Sometimes she wished she'd never shared the secret of her unusual birth with Eric and Tasha. She looked around for something to distract her friend. "Hey, look, there's a cotton-candy stand."

Amy knew Tasha had a weakness for the stuff. She could feel her own mouth water as they headed over and she watched the man swirl the paper cone in the hot spun sugar. Seeing Tasha take a nibble of the pink cloud, she couldn't resist getting one for herself. She'd just eaten the candy apple, but she couldn't amble around the carnival without some junk food in her hand.

"I'd like one too," she told the man.

He swirled another cone around and produced a cotton candy for her. Amy paid him and took the cone. "Thank you."

"Don't eat too much of this stuff," the man said. "It'll rot your teeth."

"That was a strange thing for him to say," Tasha remarked as they moved away.

"I know," Amy agreed. "Do my teeth look bad?"

"No, of course not. You've never had a cavity in your life. You're perfect, remember?"

Suddenly Amy stopped walking. "What is it?" Tasha asked eagerly. "Do you see Dwayne?"

Amy shook her head. Someone else had caught her eye. A girl, picking the last strands of pink cotton candy from a cone. She had long hair tied in a ponytail. She wore a hot-pink halter top and white shorts. But in every other way, she looked very familiar.

"Tasha . . . I think I see another Amy."

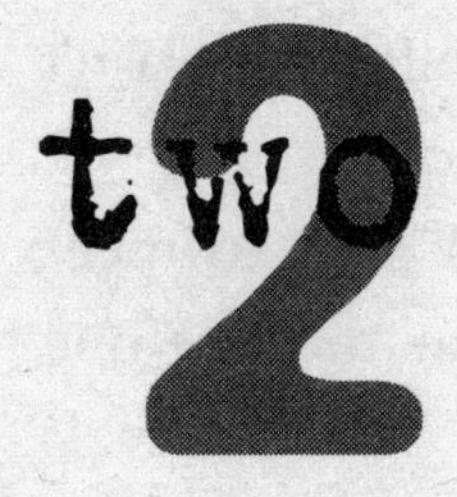

two

Amy now had Tasha's full attention. "Are you serious? Where?"

"You won't be able to see her." Amy concentrated her vision on the figure in the distance. She saw the girl toss the cotton-candy cone into a trash bin and start to walk away. A couple of other people around her blocked Amy's view for a moment. Then she caught a glimmer of hot pink.

Amy grabbed Tasha's arm. "Come on, let's go," she said. Amy knew her best friend wouldn't let her down in a situation like this, and she was right. Tasha didn't put up any resistance. They didn't run—if Amy had used her incredible athletic ability, her run would have been startlingly fast and attention-getting. But they moved swiftly through the crowds, and Amy kept her eyes peeled for that occasional glimpse of pink.

"Slow down," Tasha said, panting.

"Sorry," Amy said. The girl she was following wasn't moving quickly, so she slackened her pace.

"I don't know why you're in such a rush to meet her," Tasha declared. "Remember what the last one was like?"

Amy remembered all too well. The actress who had appeared at Parkside Middle School spelled her name Aimee, but there was no question that she was one of Amy's clones. And she'd turned out to be one of the nastiest creatures Amy had ever known.

"That doesn't mean they're all evil," Amy said. "Darn, where did she go?"

"Are you sure you saw her?" Tasha asked. "It's awfully dark and crowded. Maybe she was just a figment of your imagination."

"No way," Amy replied. "Besides, you're always telling me I *have* no imagination."

Tasha laughed. "You don't need an imagination. Your reality is weird enough. Maybe you're hallucinating."

"I never—wait, there she is, she's in line for the Ferris wheel!" They took off again. Soon they were close enough for an unobstructed view, but they kept enough distance so as not to be obvious.

"It's the girl in the pink shirt and white shorts," Amy whispered.

"The one with the ponytail?"

"Shhh," Amy hissed. "If she's an Amy, she'll hear you. What do you think? Isn't she exactly like me?"

Tasha considered the girl waiting in line. "She has a great body."

"It's no different from mine!"

"Yeah, but you don't wear shorts that tight."

Amy studied the girl. "True. My mother wouldn't let me out of the house in an outfit like that. But look at her face, Tasha. That's my face."

Tasha nodded. "I think you're right. Hey, that guy she's with is cute."

Amy hadn't noticed the people who were with the girl. Now, from the way they were standing and facing each other, she could tell that there were four kids with the clone—another girl and three boys.

"The guy with the red hair is *hot,*" Tasha declared.

"Shhh, I'm trying to hear what they're saying," Amy said.

But it wasn't possible, not even for her. There was just too much noise. Fortunately, Amy had once attended an assembly at school where a hearing-impaired speaker demonstrated sign language and lipreading. Amy had picked up both skills.

The Ferris wheel was in the process of letting riders out of their cars. As each car reached the lowest point, the wheel stopped. A couple got out, and the next two in line climbed in. The clone and her friends had reached the head of the line, and Amy could see them all moving toward the car that had just emptied. A man in a carnival T-shirt appeared to be stopping them. Amy concentrated on the man's lips.

"What do you think you're doing?"

The red-haired boy responded. "We're getting in the car. We got tickets, see?"

"Sorry, kids, only two people are allowed in each car."

"Aw, c'mon, we're a group, we want to hang together."

"Sorry," the man said again. "Two to a car, that's the rule."

Another boy, a big, dark-haired guy who looked older than the others, took over. "Don't sweat it, man, we can handle it. Let's go, guys." All five of them rushed to the car and started climbing in.

"Hey, stop that!" the man yelled.

The kids continued to pile aboard, and the red-haired boy jeered at the ride manager. "What are you going to do, call the carnival cops?" The two other boys had taken the seats, while the redhead straddled the center platform of the car. The two girls were on the boys' laps, and it was obvious that they found the whole scene hysterically funny.

People who were waiting to get on the Ferris wheel were trying to figure out what was holding up the line. And people who were already on the ride were looking down toward the ground to see why they weren't moving. Amy could see that those stuck way at the top of the wheel looked distinctly nervous.

Meanwhile, the red-haired boy had climbed off the car platform and was now straddling the metal support that connected one car to the next. The ride manager was yelling at him and trying to drag him off. The two other boys started climbing over the bar to follow the redhead onto the cable. The clone and the other girl were screaming with excitement.

"What are they doing?" Tasha asked.

"Acting silly," Amy replied. "She's got some goofy friends."

"Which means she's probably goofy too," Tasha said. "Let's get out of here, Amy. You don't want to meet her."

But now Amy was fascinated with the antics of the kids on the wheel. The ride manager blew a whistle that hung from his neck, and the shrill sound brought forth two burly men, also clad in carnival attire. The sight of these tough-looking guys must have put some fear into the group, because the redhead jumped down from the cable and the others climbed out of the car. Their spirits weren't dampened, though. They took off, running and shrieking with laughter.

As they came straight toward Tasha and Amy, Amy ducked behind her friend. She didn't want the girl discovering her until they could be alone.

So she waited until the group had raced past and then motioned to Tasha. Tasha groaned, but she stayed with Amy as Amy followed the rowdy group to the game booths.

The object of the game they chose to play had something to do with throwing sticky balls at a large tic-tac-toe board and getting three onto the board in the right pattern. One of the boys went first and couldn't get a single ball on the board. The red-haired boy went next. He wound up and pitched in a baseball style and managed to get two balls on the board. The third boy almost made it, getting two balls to stick in side-by-side squares, but his third ball fell off. Then the clone had a go at it.

"She'll blow them away," Amy whispered to Tasha. She could see that it would be relatively easy for someone with their talents to aim precisely and toss the balls with enough force to make them stick. She watched with interest as her look-alike took aim and threw.

The ball didn't even get close to the board. Her second attempt didn't produce a better result, and the third ball went careening outside the booth.

"She can't be an Amy," Tasha declared firmly. "You'd never play that badly. Even I could throw better than that."

"But she might be messing up on purpose," Amy pointed out. "Remember how I had to force myself to make mistakes in swimming class so no one would suspect that I was different?"

"I guess that's possible," Tasha said. "Maybe she's got a thing for that red-haired boy and doesn't want to outdo him. So he can feel, you know, like a guy."

"*I* never act like that," Amy said. "Ask Eric. I do lots of stuff better than him, and he doesn't care."

"Well, that guy isn't Eric," Tasha said. "And that girl isn't you."

Yes, she is, Amy said silently. No matter how badly the girl had played a carnival game of tic-tac-toe, Amy had a very strong certainty that she was looking at another Amy.

Tasha squinted. "Now what are they doing?"

"It looks like they're going to play another game . . . no, wait, that's not a game. It's some sort of contest." She concentrated on the sign and read it aloud. " 'Benefit lottery for the Bingham Children's Hospital. Win a wide-screen TV and VCR. One dollar.' " She watched as the clone handed over a dollar and filled out a form. "Look, Tasha, she has to be a nice girl. She's contributing to a charity."

"Maybe she just wants a wide-screen TV and VCR," Tasha said.

"Oh, don't be so cynical," Amy reprimanded her. "Anyone with intelligence knows that the odds of winning a lottery are, like, one in a million. And she has to be reasonably intelligent. After all, she's an Amy. I wonder what they're going to do next?"

"Are we going to be following them all night?" Tasha complained.

"I think they're leaving," Amy said. She focused on the group as they made their way toward the carnival exit. They seemed to be splitting up there. The red-haired boy got on a motorcycle, and the clone got on too. Amy watched in wonderment as her look-alike wrapped her arms around the boy's waist, the engine revved up, and they tore out into the street.

"Wow!" She told Tasha what she had just seen. "I've never been on a motorcycle before."

"Don't even think about it," Tasha said. "Your mother would kill you." She looked at Amy curiously. "How come you let her get away without making contact? I thought you were dying to meet her."

Amy grinned. She'd already thought about that. "Wait here," she instructed Tasha.

Tasha frowned.

"I'll be right back." Amy pushed her bobbed hair behind her ears so it would look like it was pulled back. She hoped the person selling the lottery tickets hadn't taken a good look at the other girl's outfit.

"Excuse me," she said to the woman at the hospital booth. "I just filled out a lottery ticket, but I think I forgot to put my phone number on it. Can I still add it?"

The woman was in the process of collecting another person's ticket. She glanced briefly at Amy's face. "You're lucky I haven't put it in the bowl yet," she murmured, and handed Amy a piece of paper before going back to the other person.

Amy read the name: Aly Kendricks. She committed the name, address, and phone number to memory. Then she returned the paper to the woman. "Thank you," she said, and turned to go back to Tasha.

Tasha wasn't alone anymore. Either she had found Dwayne, or Dwayne had found her. In any case, they were together. And Tasha had gone through a frightening transformation.

"Hi, Dwayne," Amy said. "Tasha, are you okay?" Her friend had ducked her head and was peering through her tousled curls at the handsome boy.

"I'm fine," Tasha said in a squeak about two tones higher than her natural voice. It was then that Amy realized she must be flirting. "Look what Dwayne won in the ring toss! Isn't it awesome?"

Dwayne obediently held up a plastic horn, which couldn't have been a very big prize, but Amy pretended to admire it. "Nice," she said. "Hey, aren't we supposed to meet Eric at the ring toss?"

"You go ahead," Tasha said. "I'll be there in a minute." She punctuated her words with a high-pitched giggle that Amy had never heard before. Amy looked at her in alarm, but Tasha's eyes were firmly fixed on Dwayne.

"Okay," Amy said. "Later." Hoping Tasha would recover quickly from this bout of insanity, she hurried over to the ring toss game. She found Eric there with her mother and Dr. Hopkins. "It's about time," Eric said with a scowl. "What have you been doing?"

"I was around," Amy said vaguely. She didn't want to bring up her clone sighting in front of her mother. "Mom, are you playing a game?"

Her mother grinned. "David's trying to win that big pink rabbit. He's on his third try." Amy watched as the doctor glared ferociously at the pole he was aiming at. He was holding the round hoop so tightly his knuckles were white. With a loud grunt, he threw it. The hoop hit the side of the pole and fell to the ground.

"Sorry, pal," the man at the booth said. "You want another shot at it?"

Dr. Hopkins let out a heartfelt groan. "I give up." He shook his head sorrowfully. "That rabbit would have been perfect for my waiting room."

Amy's mother gave him a sympathetic smile. "You gave it a good try."

"I could have *bought* a big pink rabbit with the money I just spent on that game," he grumbled. He was still looking with longing at the huge stuffed animal on the shelf that held the first-prize choices.

"I want to play," Amy announced. She put down some money and accepted a stack of rings from the man.

It was so easy. She simply glanced at the pole, tossed with the right amount of force, and the hoop fell neatly onto the pole. Within ten seconds she had all the hoops in the right place.

The man at the booth actually looked impressed. "What are you, little lady, some kind of ring toss professional?"

"I'll take the pink rabbit for my prize," Amy told him, and the man handed it over. "Here you go, Dr. Hopkins."

"Thanks, Amy," he said with a grin, and a couple of people who had been watching congratulated her. But she avoided her mother's eyes. She knew without looking that Nancy wouldn't approve of what she'd just done.

Her mother made her disapproval known a few minutes later when they were walking together. "Amy, you know you shouldn't show off your abilities like that. People might wonder."

Amy had heard this a zillion times, and she knew her mother was right, but this time she defended her action. "Mom, it was just a game. It's no big deal."

"Well, maybe so, but don't get carried away too often." Nancy smiled and shook her head wearily. "If you're going to use your special skills, Amy, I wish you'd reserve them for something more meaningful. Like your piano lessons."

Amy made a face. "Mom, do I have to go on taking piano? It's boring! I hate practicing those scales."

"Just stick it out for the next three months," her mother said comfortingly. "It'll get more interesting, I promise."

Amy doubted that, but she didn't argue. She had something far more fascinating to think about.

Aly Kendricks.

3 three

Getting ready for school the next morning, Amy was still thinking about the girl she'd seen the night before. As she brushed her hair and gazed at her reflection, she imagined longer hair and saw Aly Kendricks brushing hers. As she stood in front of her closet and considered what to wear, she wondered if Aly was doing the same thing. Remembering the hot-pink halter and tight white shorts, she was pretty sure Aly wouldn't be choosing the boring overalls Amy was picking out for herself. Amy probably didn't even have anything like Aly's clothes in her closet.

Impulsively Amy replaced the overalls and took out a

short pink stretchy dress instead. She'd been saving it for the next school dance, but there was no reason not to wear something a little out of the ordinary on a regular school day. She felt like being different for a change—or at least looking different. With the dress, she selected white Mary Janes instead of her usual sneakers. And she took the time to apply a little pink lip gloss.

Her mother noticed the difference. "Is there something special going on at school?" she asked at breakfast.

"No," Amy replied. "I just felt like looking hot for a change."

Nancy laughed. "You always look hot, honey. But I must say, you do look particularly hot today."

Amy wondered if Eric would notice her appearance. She was disappointed when he didn't show up to walk to school with her and Tasha. "Did he oversleep again?" she asked her best friend.

"No, he already left for school. He had to be there early."

Amy was taken aback. "For what?" She knew that only something incredibly urgent could get Eric out of bed earlier than absolutely necessary.

"He was meeting with someone who's going to tutor him in Spanish."

"He found someone overnight?" Amy was impressed. Eric was obviously serious about improving his grade.

They had just turned the corner onto the street that led to the school when a high-pitched yowling startled them. "What was *that*?" Tasha said, wincing.

Amy looked up, way up. High in the leafy branches of a tall tree, a small cat was perched on a limb and was meowing, loudly and piteously. "The poor thing, he's stuck up there," Amy told Tasha. Tasha peered up into the leaves. There was no telling how the cat had gotten himself up there, but he didn't seem to be able to come back down the same way. He made an attempt to edge down the side of the tree, started to slip, and scrambled back onto the limb.

"No way he can get down without falling," Tasha said.

"Don't cats always land on their feet?" Amy asked.

"That's a myth," Tasha replied. "He could land on his head or his back. And if he does, he's going to be killed." She was clearly distressed. "What are we going to do? We have to get him down." She made a half-hearted leap, but it was hopeless. The lowest branch was too high off the ground.

"We could call the fire department once we get to school," Amy suggested.

"He could fall before we get there," Tasha said. "Amy . . ."

"What?" Amy had a feeling she knew what Tasha was about to ask.

"I'll bet *you* could get up that tree."

"Maybe I could," Amy replied. "But I don't want to. I'm not exactly dressed for tree climbing, Tasha."

"Oh, come on, Amy," Tasha pleaded. "Look at him up there! The poor cat, he's so scared. We can't just leave him!"

Amy stared up at the animal. He did look pretty pathetic.

"He wants to go home," Tasha went on. "He wants to fill his hungry belly with tasty treats. He wants—"

Amy groaned. "Knock it off, Tasha." But she knew Tasha wouldn't. Tasha would nag her until she gave in.

"Okay, okay, I'll get him." Amy took a quick look around to make sure no one was watching; then she leaped. Grabbing the lowest limb, she swung her legs around it. The sound of ripping material told her she'd torn her dress. But there was no point in stopping now. She threw her arms around the trunk of the tree and gingerly made her way from branch to branch. A few slips along the way slowed her progress, but finally she got close enough to grab the cat.

When she had climbed back down to the ground, Tasha took the frightened animal, which immediately flew out of her arms.

"He's okay," Tasha said, watching him take off. She smiled in satisfaction. Then she turned to Amy, and her smile faded. Amy glanced down at herself and saw why. Her pink dress was streaked with dirt, and the rip in the seam went halfway up her thigh.

"You want to go home and change?" Tasha asked her.

"There's no time," Amy replied grimly. She tried to brush away some of the dirt, and Tasha produced a safety pin to keep the tear in the dress from exposing too much flesh.

But any hopes of looking hot that day evaporated. Amy spent the whole morning explaining her condition, and the more she told the story about the cat, the more annoyed she became. No one else would have even tried to climb that tree. She wondered if all the other Amys in the world had friends who took advantage of their talents. Maybe Aly Kendricks was smart enough to just say no to her friends.

"Amy Candler?"

"Here," she replied automatically, and then realized the teacher wasn't calling roll. Mr. Fitzsimmons, nicknamed Mr. Deadly Boring, was peering at her in that nearsighted way he had.

"That is not the name of the South American country which contains the largest area of the rain forest," he said. "Aren't you paying attention?"

"Yes. I mean, I am now." The class tittered, and she flushed.

"Jonathan, can you name the correct country?"

The student he called on looked blank but hazarded a guess anyway. "Argentina?"

Mr. Deadly Boring sighed heavily. "No."

Amy tried to make up for her earlier inattention. "Brazil," she said.

"That's right. And the capital of Brazil is? Anyone?"

No one responded. Deadly Boring looked at Amy.

"Brasília."

"Right. And the city with the largest population?"

Amy responded. "São Paulo."

"Correct. Now, who can name all the countries that border Brazil?"

Amy conjured up a map of South America in her head and raised her hand. It was the only hand up, so the teacher nodded at her again. She closed her eyes and began to recite.

"Colombia, Venezuela, Guyana, Suriname, French Guiana, Uruguay, Argentina, Paraguay, Bolivia, and Peru."

For a fleeting moment the teacher almost looked impressed, and Amy allowed herself a mental pat on the back. But one of the drawbacks of having superpowerful hearing skills was the fact that you could hear stuff you didn't want to hear. Like what classmates were saying behind your back.

"Candler's kissing up again."

"She's such a show-off."

"What a know-it-all."

It wasn't the whole class talking, just a few jealous jerks, but she still felt crummy. And she had to wonder if the other kids weren't having the same thoughts, even if they didn't express them.

She was glad to have French next. Other kids in that class always volunteered answers to questions, and Madame Duquesne was one of her favorite teachers. But she was in for a disappointment because Madame Duquesne was absent, and the substitute, Madame O'Reilly, had the worst French accent Amy had ever heard.

To make things more unbearable, Madame O'Reilly spent nearly half the class period reading aloud to them, and then she announced a test on what they'd just heard. All the students groaned in protest. Amy suspected that most of them had shut their brains off while the substitute had droned. That was what *she'd* done.

But unlike the others, Amy had a photographic memory, and the story Madame O'Reilly had read to them came from the textbook. Amy was able to retrieve the memory of last night's reading, and she completed the test quickly. After everyone had finished with the test, the teacher collected the papers and ordered the class to read silently while she graded them.

Amy was reading when she heard her name. "Will Amy Candler please come to my desk?"

Amy obeyed. Madame O'Reilly gazed at her through narrowed eyes. "What is the meaning of this?" she asked, tapping her fingernail on Amy's test.

Amy was confused. "Is something wrong?"

"No, nothing is wrong with your test," the teacher said. "Which means something is *very* wrong. No one else got one hundred percent. It's obvious to me that you were cheating. You must have been looking in the textbook."

Amy was outraged. "That's not true! I've never cheated in my life!"

But Madame O'Reilly wouldn't believe her. She told Amy she'd be getting a zero on the test and sent her back to her seat.

Could this day get any crummier? Thank goodness lunch was her next period and she could moan and groan to Tasha. Naturally, the cafeteria lunch was her all-time least favorite—tuna casserole. Amy dropped her tray on the table across from Tasha and began reciting her woes.

It didn't take her long to realize that her friend wasn't even listening to her. Tasha was mumbling "Mmm" every few minutes, but her eyes kept shifting to the other side of the cafeteria.

"Have you heard one word I've said?" Amy demanded.

"Sure I have," Tasha said unconvincingly. "Amy . . ."

"What?"

"You see Dwayne over there?"

Amy turned. "Yeah, I see him. Why?"

"I was just wondering if maybe you could read his lips from here and see if he's talking about me."

"Tasha!"

Tasha looked at her innocently. "What?"

"Will you please stop asking me to do stuff like that? I don't want to spy on Dwayne!"

Tasha was offended. "Well, excuse me for asking." Now she was wearing a hurt expression, and Amy wanted to scream.

She turned to see if she could read Dwayne's lips, but someone else on the other side of the room caught her eye. It was Eric. And he was sitting with a girl.

She didn't mind that Eric talked to other girls. But it was an unwritten rule, a law really, in the Parkside Middle School cafeteria—boys and girls ate at separate tables. She didn't know why the rule had begun, but it was an accepted tradition.

"Why is Eric eating lunch with Lauren Marino?" she asked Tasha.

Now Tasha got all huffy. "Oh, I see, it's okay if *I* spy for *you,* huh?"

"Okay, okay, I'll spy on Dwayne! Just tell me why Eric's sitting with Lauren!"

"Lauren's tutoring Eric in Spanish."

"Oh." It had never occurred to Amy that Eric's tutor might be the prettiest and most sophisticated girl in ninth grade.

"Now, tell me what Dwayne's saying," Tasha ordered.

Amy was forced to spend the rest of the lunch period relating Dwayne's conversation with his lunchmates. Basically, they were discussing last night's television schedule, and not one word was said about Tasha.

The rest of the school day was uneventful, not bad, but not good, either, and Amy left in a dreary mood. The fact that she had to go directly to her piano lesson didn't help.

"You're late," Mr. Lerner said when he opened the door of his house.

Amy looked at her watch. "It's only three-thirty-two!"

"Your appointment is for three-thirty."

Amy mumbled an insincere "Sorry" and took her place on the piano bench. Mr. Lerner stood just behind her, and she honestly thought she could feel his cold breath on her neck.

"Scales," he ordered.

For what must have been the zillionth time that day, Amy groaned. "Mr. Lerner, I'm so tired of doing scales. Can't I try something else?" she asked.

"You're not ready for anything else," the piano teacher said.

"But I think I am," Amy insisted. "I'll show you!" She snatched a sheet of music off the piano. Positioning her hands over the keys, she followed the notes on the sheet and hit the keys with precise accuracy.

Mr. Lerner snatched the sheet away. "Stop that!"

"Why? I wasn't making any mistakes."

"Your playing is terrible," he declared. "It's mechanical. There's no feeling, no connection. You're not ready to move on."

So it was back to the scales. And to make matters worse, Mr. Lerner informed her that once she finished the scales to his satisfaction, she had weeks and weeks more of basic exercises to look forward to.

By the time she got home that afternoon, her mood had sunk to an all-time low. And she didn't even have her mother to take it out on. This was the day Nancy taught early-evening classes at the university, and she wouldn't be home till after seven. Amy flung herself on the sofa and considered her options. She could raid the refrigerator in search of a treat, she could watch TV, she could read, or she could go next door and see what Tasha and Eric were doing.

But suddenly she knew what she really wanted to do. The big question was: Did she have the guts to do it? Before she could talk herself out of it, she leaped off the sofa and went to the kitchen phone. Lifting the receiver, she dialed the number she'd committed to memory.

A pleasant-voiced woman answered. "Hello?"

Amy hoped her voice wouldn't quiver. "Could I speak to Aly Kendricks, please?"

"Aly's not here right now, she's at Hillcrest. Do you want to leave a message?"

"No, thank you," Amy said quickly, and hung up the phone. Then she grabbed the phone book, opened it, and flipped through the pages until she reached the letter *H*.

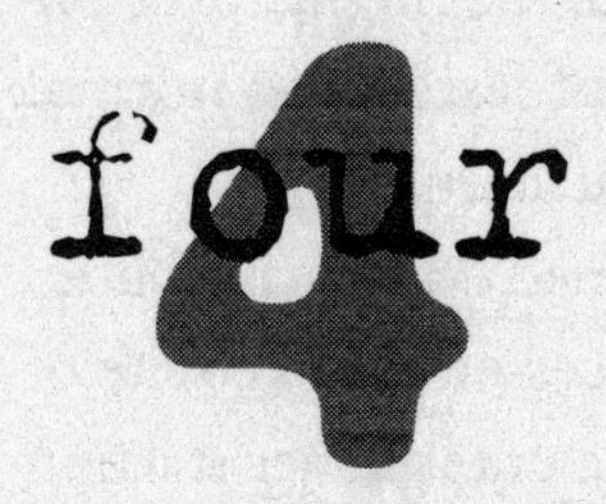

Hillcrest, Hillcrest . . . Amy ran her finger down the listings. There were about a dozen places in the phone directory that began with the word *Hillcrest*. There were Hillcrest Cinema, Hillcrest Florist, Hillcrest Laundry, Hillcrest Pharmacy . . . Her finger stopped when she reached Hillcrest Recreation Center. That was a possibility, she thought. But so was the cinema.

Then she realized that the addresses were the same for practically all the Hillcrest listings. It had to be a mall.

Rummaging through the kitchen drawers, she found a map of Los Angeles. She spread it out on the kitchen table. Using the index, she located something called Hillcrest Plaza. It was way west of where Amy lived, on the other side of the freeway and definitely not within walking distance. At least, not within normal walking distance. If she used her top speed, she might cover the distance in an hour, but that kind of faster-than-normal movement could attract unwanted attention.

She ran up to her room and turned on her computer. Logging on to the Internet, she accessed the Web site of the city transit system. Rapidly she entered her starting point and her destination, and in a couple of seconds she got a route. She'd have to change buses twice, but if she didn't have to wait too long between transfers, she could get to Hillcrest Plaza in about half an hour.

Luck was with her. Twenty-five minutes later, she was getting off the last bus, and the Hillcrest Recreation Center was spread out in front of her. It looked like a pretty big place. She went through the main door with no idea where she was going. Just inside, a reception area bore a sign: MEMBERS ONLY.

As she was trying to come up with a good excuse to get in without a membership card, the receptionist looked up. "Aren't you supposed to be in your skating class, Aly?"

"Yes," Amy said quickly. Now all she had to do was follow the signs to the rink. Once there, she settled down in a seat at the back of the audience section. Hardly any other people were watching, but there were plenty on the ice. They seemed to be divided into three groups. One group consisted of half a dozen boys and girls doing their own things. Some skated aimlessly, others twirled around, and two skated together.

The receptionist had said Aly was supposed to be in a class, and the other groups seemed more organized. In one the skaters were practicing complicated jumps, spinning twice in the air before landing. Aly wasn't among them.

Amy identified her clone in a group that was doing elementary spins. They all looked like beginners, especially Aly. While the other skaters stayed on their feet, Aly skidded across the ice. Trying again, she tripped before she could even begin the spin. On her third attempt, she fell and landed on her rear end.

Amy smiled. Aly had developed a good act. Amy remembered when she herself had first stepped onto an ice-skating rink. Never having had a lesson, she could watch a skater perform an intricate move and then, with very little effort, imitate it perfectly. Aly, of course, could do the same. But she had to know what Amy knew—that perfection would make her more noticeable, and people in their situation mustn't stand out.

Amy continued to watch. Aly was slipping and sliding

all over the ice. She didn't seem to be doing anything right, and now Amy frowned. Aly should know that it was almost as risky to be extremely bad as it was to be unusually good.

The chill from the ice reached Amy, and she shivered. She had no idea what time the class had started or what time it would be over. She didn't want to miss connecting with Aly when she left the ice, but she was cold, and since she hadn't had a snack after school she was hungry, too. She'd noticed a refreshment counter just outside the rink and hurried out.

Amy was taking her first sip of hot chocolate when she suddenly felt herself shiver again. It had nothing to do with being cold. Someone was watching her.

She turned. Immediately she knew that this had to be the first time Aly had seen one of the twelve clones. Amy remembered her own first time, when she'd spotted a ballet dancer who looked exactly like her. Aly now wore the same expression of stunned disbelief.

"Hi," Amy said. It was a pretty inadequate remark under the circumstances, but what else could she say?

For a moment Aly seemed unable to speak. Her lips moved, but no sounds came forth. Finally she managed to sputter, "Who—what—"

Amy helped her out. "I'm an Amy. Amy Candler. I'm Number Seven. Which one are you?"

There was absolutely no comprehension in the other girl's face. "You—you look just like me."

"Of course I do," Amy replied. "We all do. I've seen some of the others," she added by way of explanation.

Aly's expression was still blank. "This is very weird," she finally managed to say.

"Is your class finished?" Amy asked eagerly. "Could we go somewhere and talk?"

"We're just on a break," Aly replied. "Wait a minute. . . ." She called to a passing girl. "Carrie, tell Donna I—I have this really bad headache, okay? So I'm not coming back to class."

Fortunately, the girl didn't look at Amy as she nodded. Aly turned back to Amy. "I'm going to change clothes. Meet me outside the entrance, okay?"

Amy didn't have to wait long. When Aly appeared, she still looked like she had seen a ghost, but she was clearly excited, too. "This is so unbelievable!" she exclaimed. "What did you say your name is?"

"Amy. We were all Amy in the beginning. I guess someone changed your name."

"I'm Aly Kendricks. There's a fast-food place just inside the mall, let's go there."

The woman behind the food counter grinned at them. "Twins, huh? What would you girls like?"

They got Cokes and an order of french fries to share. "I

guess you've never met another one of us before," Amy said as they settled into a booth across from each other.

"Another person who looks just like me?" Aly shook her head. "Of course not! Have you?"

"Not *all* of them," Amy said. "But . . ." It was then that it hit her. Aly had no idea what she was talking about.

Amy tried to think of what she should say next. She had to be careful, very careful. She remembered all too well the shock of discovering the truth about herself. She didn't want to be the one to break the news to Aly Kendricks. Not yet, at least.

Aly was still clearly too excited to have noticed anything odd in what Amy had been saying. "This is really so incredible," she said, studying Amy's face. "We're identical! How tall are you? How much do you weigh?"

"Five feet exactly, one hundred pounds," Amy replied.

Aly nodded in satisfaction. "Same as me! Are you twelve years old? When were you born?"

Amy told Aly her birth date, and—if this was possible—Aly got even more excited. "That's my birthday too!" She leaned forward, her eyes shining. "Do you see what this means?"

"I'm not sure," Amy said carefully.

"We're twins! We must have been separated at birth! Wow, I thought things like that only happened in movies."

"But wouldn't our mothers have told us if we had a twin sister?"

"Mine probably didn't know," Aly said. "I was adopted."

"So was I," Amy told her. "In fact, I only learned this a few months ago. How did you find out?"

"I've known forever, as long as I can remember. My parents never tried to keep it a secret. My kid brother's adopted too. We got him when I was four." Aly grinned. "I kept asking them if they could take him back and exchange him for a girl. He's such a brat, I still wish they could! I guess it's too late for that now." She looked at Amy quizzically. "You said something about 'the others.' What did you mean?"

Amy thought quickly. "Oh, I guess I was thinking what you were thinking, about being twins separated at birth. Only I was wondering if maybe we were more like quintuplets."

"But that's pretty rare, isn't it? Anyway, I'm just so thrilled to find out I have a sister! What about you?"

"Me too," Amy said. "I'm an only child."

"Not anymore," Aly said warmly. "Wow! I know I keep saying this, but it's just so completely unbelievably unreal and amazing! Aren't you stunned?"

"It is pretty wild to find out I have a sister," Amy said, pretending to be equally surprised.

"No kidding! What's even more amazing is that we

found each other! I guess you're not from around here, or you'd be going to Hillcrest Middle School with me. Or maybe you go to a private school."

Amy shook her head. "No, I go to Parkside Middle School. I don't live anywhere near here."

"Then what were you doing in Hillcrest?"

"I saw you at the carnival this past weekend," Amy said. She explained how she'd followed Aly, and how she'd gotten her name and phone number from the lottery stand. "I called you this afternoon, and your mother said you were here. So I came to find you."

"Why didn't you just come up and speak to me at the carnival?"

"Well, you were with your friends. I didn't want to embarrass you."

"Are you kidding? Karen would have thought it was way cool."

"What about your boyfriend?" Amy asked.

"My boyfriend?" Aly asked.

"The boy with the red hair."

Aly brushed that aside. "Oh, him—he's not my boyfriend. In fact, I never saw him or those other guys before. Karen and I met them at the carnival. Do you have a boyfriend?"

"Yeah, kind of," Amy admitted. "His name is Eric Morgan."

"Lucky you," Aly said enviously. "There's a boy I like at school, but he never even looks at me."

"Eric didn't pay any attention to me for ages either," Amy assured her. "He's my best friend's brother."

"What's your best friend's name?"

"Tasha."

"Karen's my best friend." Aly paused and smiled almost shyly. "Only now that I know I have a twin sister, maybe I'll have a new best friend."

Amy smiled back. She wasn't ready to give away Tasha's title, but there was something so happy about Aly's expression that she couldn't help saying, "You never know!"

Aly was looking over Amy's shoulder now, and she waved. "Mom! Over here!"

Amy turned. A plump blond woman carrying a large shopping bag came toward their booth. With her eyes on Aly, she frowned and shook her head, but she didn't look really angry.

"What's this I just heard about a headache that was so bad you had to leave class?" she asked. "You don't look like you're in any pain to me."

Aly laughed. "I'm not. I just had to come up with an excuse to get away. Mom, look who I met!"

The woman's eyes turned to Amy, and her mouth dropped open. "Ohmigod," she gasped as she took in

Amy's resemblance to Aly. "Who are you? Where did you come from?" She sank down next to Aly in the booth and gaped at Amy. "This is remarkable! I mean, they say everyone has a twin somewhere, but you two . . . wow!"

"I think we're really twins," Aly told her. "We have the same birthday and everything. I think we were separated at birth."

"I suppose that's a possibility," her mother said. "We weren't told very much when we adopted you." A broad smile crossed her round face. "Well, isn't this something! What's your name, dear?"

"Amy. Amy Candler." Amy searched the woman's eyes for any sign of recognition at the name Amy, but there was none. Mrs. Kendricks then began asking her a barrage of questions about where she was born, her parents' names . . . but Amy didn't get to say much, because the woman looked at her watch and stopped herself. "Oh dear, look at the time, and I haven't started dinner. Where do you live, Amy? I'll drive you home."

"It's pretty far from here," Amy warned her, but Mrs. Kendricks insisted. As the girls slid out of the booth, Aly picked up her mother's shopping bag and groaned.

"This weighs a ton, Mom," she complained.

Amy studied Aly's expression. She couldn't be faking

this. She looked like she was really straining to lug the bag.

All the way home in the car, Mrs. Kendricks continued to interview Amy, but in a friendly manner that didn't make Amy feel as if she was under scrutiny. She found herself warming up to Aly's mother easily.

Once they got to Amy's neighborhood, Amy directed her through the condominium community. "It's the next right, second house on the left," she said. Then, impulsively, she asked, "Could you come in for a minute? I know you're in a rush to get home, but I really want you to meet my mother."

"Please, Mom, can we?" Aly pleaded.

Mrs. Kendricks sighed, but she smiled and nodded. "How can I say no to my daughter's twin sister?"

five 5

"I'm home," Amy called out as she opened the front door.

Her mother's voice rang out from the kitchen. "Amy, where have you been? I've been worried sick! It's almost seven-thirty, and—" She stopped speaking when she came into the entranceway and realized that Amy wasn't alone. "Oh! Hello."

Amy introduced Aly and Aly's mother. Nancy shook hands with Mrs. Kendricks and then turned to greet Aly. That was when she got her first good look at the face that was identical to her own daughter's.

Amy heard the gasp her mother barely managed to

stifle. Mrs. Kendricks chuckled in response to the surprise on Nancy Candler's face. "Isn't this remarkable?" she crowed. "I have to say, I was absolutely floored when I saw your daughter! Have you ever seen such a close resemblance?"

There was a slight quiver in Nancy's voice as she responded. "It's certainly a remarkable resemblance. Please, come sit down and have something to drink." She ushered them all into the big kitchen, where Dr. Hopkins was already sitting at the table. He rose as Nancy introduced the guests, and there was no mistaking the shock on his face when he saw Aly and Amy together. He recovered quickly, shaking hands with Mrs. Kendricks, but he couldn't keep his eyes off Aly.

"You're a doctor?" Mrs. Kendricks asked. "Well, maybe you can come up with some medical explanation for this!"

"No, I—I don't think I can," Dr. Hopkins said.

"Oh, who cares how this happened?" Mrs. Kendricks said gaily. "It's a happy coincidence, that's all! It's just pure luck that they found each other."

Her cheerful acceptance of this so-called coincidence was in stark contrast to the reaction on Nancy's face. Amy watched her mother's eyes dart nervously between Amy and Aly.

"Actually, it was Amy who found me," Aly said. "She saw me at the carnival last weekend."

"Well, that's no surprise," her mother said. "I'm sure you weren't wearing your glasses."

Dr. Hopkins looked at Aly with extreme interest. "You wear glasses?"

"Poor child, she can barely see farther than three feet in front of her," Mrs. Kendricks reported.

"Oh, Mom, I'm not *that* blind," Aly remonstrated. To Amy she said, "I look totally gross with glasses on. And I can't wear contacts because of my allergies. My eyes get too itchy. Do you have bad eyesight?"

"No, my eyes are fine," Amy admitted.

"Well, that's one thing that's different about us," Aly said. "I'll bet you don't have allergies, either."

"No, no allergies."

"Lucky you."

"Would you like some coffee or tea?" Nancy asked Mrs. Kendricks. "How about you, Aly? Some juice, a Coke?"

Mrs. Kendricks answered for both of them. "No, thank you, we must be going. I'm sure we'll be seeing each other again soon. I have a feeling we won't be able to keep these two apart!"

Aly looked at Amy eagerly. "I'm having a sleepover on Friday. Want to come?"

"I'd love to!" Amy replied promptly. "Can I, Mom?"

Nancy glanced uneasily at Dr. Hopkins. "I'm not sure . . ."

"It's perfectly fine with me," Mrs. Kendricks assured her. "Aly's having four of her friends, and one more is no bother. My husband and I will be home, of course, so the girls can't get into too much trouble!"

Nancy twisted her hands together. She didn't look too thrilled at the prospect, but what possible reason could she come up with to say no? "Well . . . I suppose that's all right."

There was an exchange of phone numbers, and then Amy and her mother followed Mrs. Kendricks and Aly to the door. Amy stepped outside to wave as they got into their car.

"See you on Friday!" Aly called.

"Friday!" Amy echoed happily. She watched the car drive away. And then she had to go back inside and face her mother.

Nancy Candler was clearly distressed. "Now, what was *that* all about?"

Amy couldn't fake innocence. Nancy knew her too well. "Like Aly said, I saw her at the carnival. I figured she had to be another Amy from Project Crescent, so I wanted to meet her."

Dr. Hopkins frowned. "Amy, you know it could be

dangerous for the Project Crescent clones to get involved with each other. The organization could still be watching you."

"Only now I know she can't be a clone," Amy went on. "Not if she's got allergies and wears glasses. And you should have seen her ice-skating. No one could fake being that bad! It has to be like Mrs. Kendricks said, just a weird coincidence, right? So there's no reason why we can't be friends."

But her mother and Dr. Hopkins were looking at each other in a way she didn't like. She waited, but neither said anything.

Amy pressed them. "She's not one of the twelve clones, right?"

Dr. Hopkins nodded at Nancy, and Nancy spoke. "There weren't twelve clones, Amy. There were thirteen."

"Thirteen," Amy repeated. *"Thirteen?"* This was unreal. Here she'd been believing she knew everything about her bizarre background. Apparently not. She glared at her mother and waited for further explanation. Dr. Hopkins broke in with a long, complicated discussion of gene splitting and cell structure and spontaneous regeneration. What it all came down to was that the scientists had cultivated twelve genetically designed embryos, just as Amy had been told, but in the way that ordinary twins evolve, one of the embryos had divided.

"We observed them both," Nancy told her, "and one of the divided embryos—Amy, Number Twelve—developed as we'd expected, in a manner identical to the first eleven. But in the thirteenth, the DNA was different. We could never explain why; it was an accident of nature, a genetic fluke. And when Amy, Number Thirteen, reached the fetal stage, we could ascertain that she wouldn't have the genetic perfection of the others."

Dr. Hopkins picked up the story. "We didn't know what to do. The organization funding the experiment was only interested in perfect clones. Dr. Jaleski assumed that Number Thirteen would be destroyed."

Amy's hand flew to the pendant she always wore around her neck. It was a little silver crescent moon, and it had been given to her by Dr. Jaleski just before he died. She couldn't believe that the kind man, the director of Project Crescent, would destroy an innocent imperfect child.

She was right.

"Dr. J wouldn't do it," her mother said. "But he knew we had to dispose of the infant before the organization learned about her. He arranged for some sort of secret adoption. He never told us where, or who took the infant. He thought it would be safer for us not to know, in case the organization somehow discovered her existence."

Amy absorbed this new information. "And that's Aly? The thirteenth Amy?"

"It's possible," Dr. Hopkins admitted. "The physical resemblance is extraordinary, and she obviously doesn't have your capabilities."

Nancy's eyes were dark with concern. "I don't think it's a good idea for you and Aly to become close friends, Amy. It could be dangerous for you. And her, too."

"Why?"

"The organization still exists, Amy. You know that. But we don't know what they know, or what they're capable of learning. This situation could interest them."

Amy tried to not to show her impatience. Nancy saw danger around every corner. Personally, Amy sometimes thought her mother was a little paranoid.

And though Amy knew she had been under surveillance, she didn't believe the organization was interested in her anymore. It had been ages since she'd felt directly threatened. And so Nancy's words depressed her.

"Mom, I like her. I want to be her friend."

Her mother sighed. "I guess I don't have any real reason to forbid you to see her. But please, sweetie, be very careful. Don't give Aly or her family any reason to believe that the two of you have anything more in common than an unusual resemblance."

"I won't," Amy promised. She had absolutely no desire to show off her skills to this new friend. She didn't want to be known as someone with extraordinary talents. She wanted Aly to think she was one hundred percent ordinary.

Amy was dying to tell Tasha and Eric about Aly. So as soon as dinner was finished, she rushed next door. But Eric wasn't home, and Tasha wasn't alone. Dwayne was with her on the living room floor, books and papers spread out around them. Tasha looked supremely happy as she greeted Amy. "We're doing homework together," she explained.

Amy tried very hard not to roll her eyes. "That's nice. What are you working on?"

"Romeo and Juliet," Dwayne said. "It's a play by William Shakespeare."

No kidding, Amy replied silently. But it had to be big

news to Dwayne, who had probably never heard of Shakespeare before. "It's a great play," she said.

He looked skeptical. "Yeah? I think it's weird. It doesn't make much sense." He read from the book. " 'A rose by any other name would smell as sweet.' What's that supposed to mean?" He looked at Tasha.

"Gee, I'm not sure," Tasha said. "It does sound kind of weird."

Amy wanted to scream. Tasha knew perfectly well what that sentence meant. English was her best subject. She was simply playing dumb for Dwayne's sake.

Just then the phone rang, and a second later Tasha's mother appeared. "Hi, Amy. Dwayne, that was your mother on the phone. You were supposed to be home at eight o'clock."

"What time is it now?" he asked.

"Try looking at your watch," Amy suggested.

He did, and said, "Wow, it's almost nine."

"Gee, you can tell time," Amy murmured. Tasha shot her an evil look. And as soon as Dwayne had left, she practically exploded at Amy.

"Why are you so nasty to him?" she demanded. "He's never been mean to you."

"I know, I know," Amy said. "But I just don't get it. How can you like him? There's nothing between his ears!"

Tasha glared at her dangerously. "Just because he's not some sort of mutant genetic genius . . ."

Amy glared right back. "He's not even normally intelligent, Tasha. And why are you acting like you're stupid too? Since when do you have trouble understanding *Romeo and Juliet*? You practically know that play by heart!"

Tasha couldn't deny that. "I just don't want Dwayne to feel bad about not getting it."

"So you're going to pretend you're even dumber than he is? Tasha, you can't have an honest relationship if you don't act like yourself!"

"I thought you didn't want me to have a relationship with him at all!" Tasha shot back.

Amy let out a long, weary sigh. "Oh, Tasha, let's not fight. Look, if you really like Dwayne, I won't say anything. But just be yourself, okay? Anyway, I've got something to tell you." But before she could embark on her story, the door opened and Eric came in. And *he* wasn't alone.

Beautiful Lauren Marino was laughing at something, tossing her head so her glossy black curls bounced on her shoulders. "Oh, Eric, you're too funny!"

Eric was looking very pleased with himself. It took him a minute to get his eyes off Lauren long enough to greet Amy. "Hi. Do you know Lauren?"

Amy and Lauren exchanged hellos, and then Eric said, "Lauren and I have been at the library, working on Spanish."

He sounded like he was making some sort of excuse, and Amy looked at him suspiciously. "That's nice," she said.

Eric didn't pick up on her expression or her tone. Now he was offering Lauren something to drink, and Tasha was complimenting the older girl on her rose-colored sweater twinset. Amy decided there was no reason to hang around anymore. She couldn't tell her story with this other girl there anyway.

Back home, Amy's mother and Dr. Hopkins were still talking at the dinner table. Amy went up to her room.

She didn't have any homework, and it was too early to go to bed. So she picked up her extension phone and dialed.

"Aly, hi, it's Amy Candler! I'm not calling too late, am I?"

Aly sounded happy to hear from her. "No, I was just watching *Dateline* on TV."

"You like that show?" Amy asked doubtfully. She wasn't crazy about those newsmagazine programs. The subjects were usually pretty depressing.

"No, I hate it, it's so depressing," Aly replied. "But

there was a story about welfare reform, and that's what we're studying in social studies, so our teacher said we had to watch it."

"My mother hates it when a teacher assigns us a TV show," Amy remarked. "She says we watch enough TV already."

"Yeah, my dad says the same thing. But it's not like they ever assign us anything good to watch anyway."

"No kidding," Amy agreed. "Just once I'd like to hear my teacher tell us we have to watch *Buffy*."

"That's my favorite show!" Aly exclaimed. "Do you like *Dawson's Creek*?"

"It's okay," Amy said. "Those kids are always whining and complaining about everything. They annoy me sometimes."

"That is so true," Aly declared. "I used to love Joey, but even she's starting to get on my nerves. Hold on a second." Amy heard her yell, "Okay, okay."

"Do you have to go?" Amy asked.

"Nah, that was my mother. She was just telling me there's some stupid figure skating competition on another channel."

Amy was surprised at her tone. "You don't like figure skating?"

"No, I'm only taking the lessons because my mother

used to be a skater. She just wants me to give it a chance. She says if I still hate it after three months I can quit."

Amy was delighted. "That's the same deal I have with my mother about piano lessons!"

After that, they couldn't stop comparing stuff. They discovered they both loved swimming and hated volleyball. Both of them wanted the new super-high platform shoes that were in all the magazines, but they'd both been forbidden to get them because they were supposed to be bad for your ankles. They both liked Backstreet Boys better than 'N Sync, and they both thought Britney Spears was just so-so. And they both absolutely loved Will Smith.

"I even watch him on the reruns of that TV show he used to be on," Aly said.

"So do I," Amy replied, "but I like him better as a singer."

"Yeah, me too."

Eventually Nancy realized that Amy was on the phone and called to her to get off. And Aly's mother was still bugging her to come watch the skating show.

"I'll call you tomorrow night," Aly said.

"Okay, and I can't wait for Friday."

"Yeah, it'll be cool. Bye!"

Hanging up, Amy lay back on her bed in contentment. It seemed like ages since she'd last had a good conversation with a friend. She used to talk with Tasha like this all the time. But if Tasha insisted on acting like someone other than herself, Amy thought she might have to find a new best friend. And while Aly wasn't a perfect Amy clone, she just might be a perfect pal.

7 seven

"Lovely house," Amy's mother murmured as she parked the car at the curb in front of the address Mrs. Kendricks had given them. Amy agreed. The Kendricks home wasn't a mansion like the houses in nearby Beverly Hills, but it was certainly a lot bigger than Amy's home. It was a wide, two-story colonial-style house, shaded by big, leafy trees and set way back from the street behind an expanse of neatly cut green grass. On the lawn, a chubby, practically bald man with a fuzzy white beard was tossing a baseball to a skinny boy in baggy jeans.

"That must be Aly's father," Nancy said.

"He looks like Santa Claus," Amy remarked. She didn't think it was a bad way to look. In fact, he seemed to fit into the cheerful scene very well.

Aly must have been watching from the window, because as soon as Amy and her mother got out of the car, she flew out the front door and ran toward them. It felt a little strange for Amy to be hugging a girl she'd only met once before, but they'd been on the phone every night since. And besides, it wasn't like Aly was an ordinary new friend. These were special circumstances.

Aly introduced them to the people on the lawn. "That's my father, that's my brother, Ricky." Obviously, she had prepared them for the amazing resemblance between the two girls, since neither did a major double take, though Ricky did slap his head in an exaggerated manner and moan, "Oh, no, two of her!" He looked like a typical nine-year-old boy.

Mr. Kendricks gave them a big, warm smile that made him look even more like Santa Claus. Now Mrs. Kendricks was waving from the front door and inviting them in. Nancy begged off—she had an appointment—but she was clearly reassured to see that Amy would be spending the night among such nice people.

"Have fun and behave yourself and don't make problems for the Kendricks," she said to Amy. Lowering her voice, she added, "And don't do anything—well, you know what I mean."

Amy nodded wearily. Did her mother really think she was dying to show off her unique qualities to every person who crossed her path? Didn't her mother have any idea how much Amy appreciated being with people who didn't know she was different?

Aly tugged at Amy's arm. "Come on, I want to show you my room." They started toward the house as Mr. Kendricks and Ricky resumed throwing the ball back and forth. Amy turned to wave politely and call out, "Nice to meet you," at the very moment that Ricky fumbled his throw. The ball took off in an unintended direction—directly toward the girls. In a split second, Amy could see that given the speed of the ball and the pace at which they were walking, the ball would smack right into the back of Aly's head.

She had to move just as fast—so fast she knew she might look like an unnatural blur to Mr. Kendricks and his son. But she had to risk that for Aly's sake. She threw herself into the path of the ball and caught it just before it would have struck Aly.

In the commotion that followed, with Aly's shrieking at Ricky, Ricky's apologies, and Mr. Kendricks's exclamations of concern, no one made a big deal about

Amy's amazing reflexes. Mr. Kendricks did thank her for stepping in so quickly, and he commented on her quick thinking and action.

"It was just a lucky catch," Amy said, and thank goodness, he didn't challenge that. But they were all looking at her with serious admiration, and she felt a little uncomfortable. She was always having to remind herself to watch out in situations like this.

Inside the house, Amy wasn't surprised to see that it was cozy and inviting, just like the entire Kendricks family.

"My room's in the basement," Aly said, and she led Amy through the kitchen to a door that opened onto a staircase. The downstairs wasn't like any basement Amy had ever seen before. It wasn't a dark cement dungeon, with exposed pipes or old broken furniture lying around. The Kendrickses' basement had been painted a bright, cheery yellow. High windows let in plenty of light.

And it was *huge*! "It's more like an apartment than a bedroom," Amy marveled. At one end of the room were a sofa and chairs; a television and a stereo; shelves filled to overflowing with board games, compact discs, and magazines; and a desk with a large computer and a stack of the latest computer games. There was even a mini-refrigerator, which Aly opened to display cans and bottles of every imaginable soft drink and juice.

At the other end of the room were bunk beds, a dresser, and the biggest doll house Amy had ever seen. "Of course, I don't play with it anymore," Aly hastened to explain. "But I still like to have it around."

"It's fantastic," Amy said, admiring the miniature furniture inside.

"My father made it," Aly told her proudly. "He's really good with his hands. He can fix just about anything too. He used to be a carpenter. Then he started a repair business, and now he's got a whole staff of people who go out to fix stuff."

"I'll have to tell my mother that," Amy said. "We always have things in our place that need fixing. My mother can barely change a lightbulb."

"Are your parents divorced?" Aly wanted to know.

Amy hesitated. For one wild and crazy moment, she had an urge to tell Aly the real story. But of course, she couldn't. So she gave her the same made-up story she told everyone, the same story her mother had told her before she knew the truth. "My father was killed in an accident just before I was born," she said.

Aly frowned. "But you said you were adopted, like me."

Amy could have kicked herself. She had to get her story straight. "I meant, just before I was adopted." Quickly she changed the subject. "This is really a super room, Aly."

Aly nodded happily. "And it's great for sleepovers. The sofa pulls out to become a double bed and the pillows are big enough to sleep on too. We can make as much noise as we want, too, because my parents can't hear a thing."

That was fortunate for Aly's parents. Aly's other sleepover guests began to arrive, and one by one, each of them screamed as she saw that Amy looked exactly like Aly.

"If you got your hair cut, you two could be twins," one girl said.

"I think maybe we *are* twins," Aly said. "And we were separated at birth."

"Or it could be just a coincidence," another girl remarked. "People constantly think I'm the figure skater Tara Lipinski."

Aly nodded. "My mother says that everyone in the world has someone else who looks exactly like them. But I still feel like I found a sister." She grinned at Amy, and Amy felt warm all over.

She liked Aly's friends, too. Karen, Aly's best friend, was petite, with long, straight light brown hair, and she *did* look like Tara Lipinski. The others—Amber, Melissa, and Courtney—didn't look like anyone famous, but they were all cute and fun. Melissa was absolutely enthralled by the possibilities of having a twin.

"Think of the tricks you two could play on people! Are you good in math, Amy?"

"I'm okay," Amy admitted.

"Then you could take math tests for Aly! It's her worst subject."

"I'm not that bad," Aly protested. "But I like the idea! And I'm pretty good in science projects, so I could do those for Amy."

Amy knew that Aly couldn't be better at anything than she was, but of course she kept that to herself. She thought of something else that could be funny, though. "Maybe you could get together with my boyfriend, Eric. I'd love to see if he could tell the difference between us!"

It was a great evening. Courtney was a cheerleader, and she taught them all a silly dance routine. They gorged on pizzas, they danced to music blasting from the stereo, and they watched a scary video that had them all screaming. After that, they watched everyone's all-time favorite movie, *Grease,* and they sang—or shrieked—all the songs together. By midnight Amy felt like she'd known all these girls forever. And no one was ready for bed.

There were a variety of suggestions as to what they could do next—everything from dying their hair with Kool-Aid to making prank phone calls—but Aly came up with the best idea. "Let's go for a swim!"

Amy hadn't seen anything that looked like a swimming pool around the Kendricks home. "Where?"

"Next door," Aly told her. "The neighbors have a pool, and they're out of town. We can climb over the fence."

"We don't have bathing suits," Karen reminded her.

But Aly had several bathing suits, plus leotards. Before long they were all tiptoeing out the back door of the house. Aly was just behind Amy, and she whispered in her ear.

"Amy, is that a tattoo on your back?"

Amy knew what she was talking about: the small image of a crescent moon. Back in the laboratory, twelve years ago, all the Amy clones had been marked that way.

"It's a birthmark," she said. "Don't you have one?"

"No. I guess we're not completely identical." Aly sounded almost disappointed.

Amy tried to make a joke of it. "Well, at least we'll be able to tell each other apart." And she supposed it was a good thing. The mark would always remind her of how she was different from Aly, in a much more serious way.

Still, as she climbed over the fence and jumped into the warm pool with the others, it was nice to be able to forget about that difference for a while. And it was so easy with this group of new friends. Unlike some others, they didn't expect her to be perfect.

"This water feels wonderful," she told Aly. "It's so warm."

"It's heated," Aly told her.

"Really? The people leave the heat on even when they're out of town?"

The same thought hit her and Aly at the same time. Simultaneously they gasped. And at that very minute, a light went on in the house behind them, a window opened, and an angry voice yelled, "Who's out there? What's going on?"

The girls scrambled out of the pool with muffled shrieks and giggles. Frantically they got over the fence, back into the Kendrickses' house, and down to Aly's basement room. There they waited nervously for a few minutes to see if the neighbor was going to come after them. When nobody came, they collapsed on the floor in hysterical laughter.

After the adventure, they were all starving. Aly produced chips, dips, and cookies, and they pigged out. And after that, they all dropped in exhaustion.

Climbing up the ladder to the bunk bed above Aly, Amy couldn't remember ever having had so much fun in one evening. And what made it really, truly special was the fact that she'd had a wild and crazy adventure without doing anything extraordinary, without using any special skills or talents. She'd had silly, reckless fun in the same normal way as everyone else.

She dropped off to sleep almost immediately. But she woke up soon after and realized she was feeling a cold draft. It was coming from an open window.

She didn't bother with the ladder to get down from the bunk. Silently she dropped down and looked around the dark basement room. There had to be some kind of pole with a hook that Aly used to open and close the high windows, but she didn't see it lying around. If she started searching, she might wake up the others. In any case, she really didn't need the pole.

She positioned herself just far enough from the window to build momentum. Then she ran, did a flying leap, reached the window, and pushed it shut. Landing on her toes, she was pleased at having been able to accomplish the little mission silently.

But not quite silently enough. A soft, groggy voice mumbled from the bottom bunk. "How did you do that?"

Amy froze. Aly's eyes were just slightly open, and

Amy knew she couldn't see too clearly in the dark room. Amy took a chance. "You're dreaming," she whispered.

"Oh." Aly closed her eyes.

Amy watched her for a minute, until she was sure Aly was sleeping again. She was tempted to leap up to her top bunk, but she didn't. She climbed the ladder like a normal person.

eight 8

"What's so great about that?" Tasha wanted to know when Amy finished reporting the events of the sleepover on the phone. "So Aly and her friends think you're an ordinary person—big deal. Remember when you had that awful fever and you really lost your powers? You were totally ordinary then, and you weren't very happy about it."

It was Sunday morning, and this was the first chance Amy had had to call Tasha. The sleepover girls had slept late on Saturday and spent the rest of the day fooling around back at the carnival. By the time Amy had returned home Saturday night, she'd been too wiped out to do anything but crash and dream about the good time she'd had.

But Tasha wasn't getting it. She couldn't understand why the sleepover had been so much fun for Amy.

Amy tried to explain. "It's not that I want to lose my powers. It's just nice to have friends who don't expect me to do special things for them all the time."

"Who asks you to do special things for them all the time?" Tasha asked.

"Well . . . you do."

"I do not!"

"You wanted me to look for Dwayne at the carnival," Amy reminded her. "You asked me to read his lips to find out if he was talking about you."

"Well, excuse me!" Tasha said in a huffy voice. "I didn't realize what kind of terrible burden I was putting on you."

Now Amy felt bad. She hadn't meant to offend Tasha. "Listen, what are you doing today?"

"Why?" Tasha asked.

"I'm meeting Aly and her friend Karen at the mall. We're going to hang out there all day."

"And do what?"

Amy frowned. Couldn't Tasha grasp the concept of just hanging out? Aly and her buds seemed to do this all the time, and Amy hadn't had all that much difficulty understanding the activity. "I don't know, just hang out. Shop, have lunch. Maybe go to a movie. Want to come?"

Tasha hemmed and hawed, but since she didn't have anything else to do, she finally agreed.

An hour later Amy knocked at Tasha's door to collect her.

Tasha, though, wasn't ready to leave just yet. And Amy was alarmed to find Dwayne parked in front of the TV in Tasha's living room. "He's not coming with us, is he?" she whispered in Tasha's ear.

"No, he just came by to bring me a book I wanted to borrow," Tasha replied.

Amy couldn't resist a shocked expression. "A book? Dwayne Hicks reads *books*?" As she spoke, she noticed that Tasha seemed to be holding something behind her. Sure enough, Tasha edged backward and dropped the item on a table. Amy got a good look at it.

"A comic book? Since when do you read comic books?"

"It's *Alien Avenger,*" Tasha replied defensively. "Dwayne says it's really good. Right, Dwayne?"

"Huh?" Dwayne's eyes didn't stray from the TV screen.

"*Alien Avenger* is better than ordinary comic books, right?"

"Yeah, and there's a computer game that goes with

it. It's totally awesome. I've been saving up my allowance for it, and I think I'm going to get it this week. We can play it next weekend."

Tasha uttered that new high-pitched giggle that Amy found so annoying. "Ooh, I'm terrible at computer games, everything happens so *fast*! You're going to have to help me with it, Dwayne."

"No problem," Dwayne said.

Tasha noticed Amy's expression. She whispered softly so Dwayne couldn't hear her. "Amy, if you roll your eyes one more time, they're going to fall out of their sockets."

"Sorry," Amy whispered back. "Hi, Dwayne."

The gorgeous dummy gave her a gorgeous dumb grin and then turned back to the TV, where a movie was showing. Amy looked at the screen. A figure completely wrapped in dirty rags was staggering ominously toward a woman who huddled in a corner and screamed.

"What's that?" she asked.

"The Mummy's Girlfriend," Dwayne answered. "See, she just said the magic words that released the mummy from the tomb where he's been buried for a thousand years. Now he's coming after her because he thinks she's his chick. He wants to take her back into the tomb with him."

"So why is she just sitting there?" Amy wanted to know. "That's what I hate about these movies. The woman just hangs around and cries instead of fighting back or running."

Dwayne looked at her blankly, as if he didn't understand what she was talking about, so Tasha replied for him. "It's more scary this way." She gave a delicate shudder. "It's *too* scary for me!" She put her hands over her eyes. "I can't watch anymore, it's so creepy! Dwayne, please, turn it off!"

Dwayne obliged. "I have to go now anyway," he said. He gave Tasha a kindly smile. "Don't get upset, it's only a movie. I don't think real mummies can ever come back to life like that."

Tasha gazed at him adoringly. Amy resisted the urge to gag.

She tried to be fair. Dwayne wasn't a bad guy, and he was acting like he really cared about Tasha. If Tasha liked him, Amy would just have to accept him. What she couldn't accept was the way Tasha was behaving, so *not* like herself.

Somehow, during the long bus ride to the mall, Amy managed to keep quiet about Dwayne. She used the time to regale Tasha with more detailed stories of the sleepover.

Tasha didn't think the pool incident was funny.

"That wasn't a very nice thing to do to Aly's neighbors," she commented.

Amy defended their actions. "We didn't do any damage. All we did was splash around in their pool."

"But it wasn't your pool," Tasha argued. "Would you consider breaking into the neighbors' house?"

"Of course not!"

"So what's the difference between doing that and going in their pool? It's the same thing."

"No, it isn't," Amy said.

"Yes, it is," Tasha replied.

This argument was going nowhere, and Amy didn't want to continue it. "We were just having a good time," she muttered. She glanced at Tasha and hoped her friend wasn't going to spend the afternoon lecturing Aly and Karen about proper behavior.

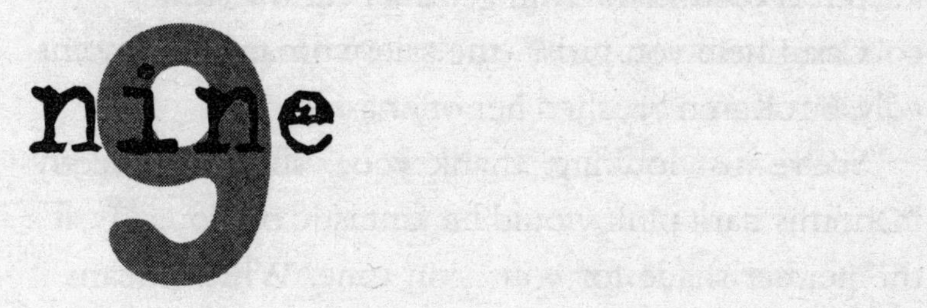

Tasha got along fine with the girls—at least, for about the first thirty minutes, when they wandered around looking in store windows and pointing out what they'd like to have but couldn't afford to buy.

In a large department store, Aly lit up as they passed through the cosmetics section. "Let's do makeovers!" she proposed.

"This stuff is really expensive," Tasha pointed out.

"We'll just use the samples," Aly assured her.

Tasha was still concerned. "Won't they get mad if we don't buy anything?"

Neither Aly nor Karen seemed to have any worries.

But Amy noticed the saleswoman's expression as they surrounded the elaborate display of cosmetics on the counter. The woman had to know that a bunch of preteens wouldn't be making any purchases, and they'd keep real customers from getting near the stuff.

"Can I help you girls?" the saleswoman asked pointedly, but Karen brushed her offer aside.

"We're just looking, thank you," she said sweetly. "Oh, this dark pink would be fantastic on you, Aly, it's the perfect shade for your skin tone. Which means it would be great on you, too, Amy."

"Karen knows everything about makeup," Aly told Amy and Tasha. "Her mother works at a beauty spa. What about Tasha, Karen? What color should she wear?"

"No thanks," Tasha said quickly. She seemed to be wilting under the annoyed gaze of the saleswoman. But the hard looks weren't bothering Aly.

"Karen, do me and Amy together with the same makeup," she proposed.

Karen was happy to oblige. She started with their eyes, using thick black liner and navy blue shadow. While the saleswoman glared at them with increasing hostility, Karen proceeded to apply mascara, blush, and iridescent highlights. As the look-alikes were covered with makeup, the counter was covered with speckles of powder and drops of creams. And now the saleswoman was speaking angrily into a telephone.

"I think she's calling security," Tasha said nervously.

"I don't think we're doing anything against the law," Amy mumbled in response. She couldn't speak very well because Karen was in the process of outlining her lips in a violent shade of lavender. She did the same to Aly and then filled in both sets of lips with an even deeper purple color.

"Finished!" she declared, and pulled both girls toward the mirror on the counter. "How do you like it?"

"It's fabulous!" Aly squealed. "We look at least eighteen!"

Amy could agree with the latter part of Aly's reaction. She wasn't so sure she considered their look fabulous, but she tried to look as enthusiastic as Aly.

"It's very cool, Karen," she declared. "Tasha, what do you think?"

For once Tasha was incapable of faking anything. "You look kind of silly," she said bluntly.

Amy glanced at Aly to see how she was taking this comment. But Aly just laughed. "It's wild and crazy," she acknowledged. "And I love it!"

"Me too!" Amy added quickly. They posed together

in front of the mirror, gesturing dramatically, while Karen roared with laughter.

Suddenly a woman in uniform appeared before them. "I'm going to have to ask you girls to leave this counter at once," she announced. "You're disturbing the other customers."

"That's okay, we're finished," Karen said impudently, and they all ran out of the store laughing. At least, Amy, Aly, and Karen were laughing. Tasha dragged along behind them.

"Want to see what's playing at the multiplex?" she asked hopefully.

But Aly had stopped walking, right in front of a hair salon. "I just had the most brilliant idea. My mother gets her hair cut here, and the manager knows her. I'll bet she'd cut my hair for me and charge it to my mother."

"You never said you wanted to get your hair cut," Karen said, but Aly had already gone into the salon. The others followed.

The manager did recognize Aly. "Good grief! Your mother never said she had twins!"

Aly laughed in delight. "She didn't know, and neither did I!" She gave the woman a brief rundown of the situation. "Could I get a haircut right now? My mother will pay when she comes in on Wednesday."

Luckily, a stylist was available. Aly went into the bathroom to change into the salon's special robe. Then she came out and sat in the stylist's chair.

"How do you want your hair cut?" the stylist asked.

"Exactly like hers," Aly said, pointing to Amy.

Aly was shampooed, and the stylist went to work with the scissors. Once she'd finished and began blowing Aly's hair dry, Amy got her own brilliant idea. "I'll be right back," she told the others, and ran out of the salon. There was a hip clothing store just opposite the salon, and she went in.

She made her purchases, noting that she would have very little money left, but she didn't care. She went back to the salon.

Aly was admiring herself in the mirror. Amy stood by her side. "Ohmigod," Aly breathed. "Now we're *totally* identical."

Amy disagreed. "Not totally. Not yet." She motioned for Aly to come with her into the bathroom. They emerged wearing Amy's purchases.

Now it was Karen's turn to murmur "Ohmigod," and Tasha too was gaping at them. In their identical light blue T-shirts and dark denim jeans, there was no way anyone could tell them apart. It was a happy coincidence that they'd both worn white sneakers that day—Amy couldn't have afforded two pairs of new shoes.

Aly was ecstatic. She pulled out her wallet so she could pay Amy back. "But I don't think I'm going to have enough left for a movie now," she said. She started to count her change. Then she frowned and started counting over. "I always get confused when I'm trying to count money," she murmured.

"I can't add either," Amy assured her, avoiding Tasha's look. As it turned out, Aly didn't have enough money left for a movie ticket. Tasha and Karen together didn't have enough money left to buy more than one ticket each.

"Wait a minute," Aly said. Her eyes were sparkling. "We only need three tickets for the four of us." She explained her new brilliant idea to the others.

Tasha was horrified. "But that's stealing!"

Aly could roll her eyes exactly like Amy. "Oh, don't be so prissy!"

Tasha drew her breath in sharply and stepped back. She said nothing, but Amy could see the hurt in her eyes.

"Okay," Amy said quickly, "let's go." She wasn't exactly comfortable with the plan, but she went along with it.

"I'm going in," Tasha said shortly as they got to the multiplex.

"Save us seats," Aly called after her as Tasha bought

her ticket and went into the theater. Then Aly turned to Amy. "Which part do you want to play?"

Wanting Aly to think she was really into this, Amy volunteered for the more dangerous role. Aly went into action. First she gave Amy her eyeglass case. Then she went to the booth, bought a ticket, and stuck it in her pocket. At the door of the theater, where she was supposed to give the ticket to the ticket taker, she pretended she couldn't find it.

"I know I've got it here somewhere," she said, searching in her bag. As Amy and Karen watched from behind a pillar, Aly fussed and moaned and made sure that the ticket taker was getting a good look at her. She pretended to be surprised and relieved when she found the ticket in her pocket and handed it over. Then she went into the theater.

Karen then bought her ticket and went in. Amy waited for three minutes, as Aly had instructed her to do, and tried to ignore the pounding of her heart. It was ironic, in a way. She'd been in much more dangerous situations in the past, hiding from the organization and escaping from those who were working for the evil group. But for some reason, this little escapade made her more nervous.

Finally she hurried to the theater. When she reached

the ticket taker, she pretended to be out of breath and waved Aly's glasses in his face. "I forgot my glasses!" she cried out. "Remember me? I already gave you a ticket."

The ticket taker nodded, and Amy went on into the theater. The ruse had worked.

The previews were already on, so the lights were down, but Amy spotted Aly and Karen waiting for her. "Where's Tasha?"

"We couldn't find her," Aly said. "She probably didn't save us seats anyway. What's her problem? Doesn't she like to have fun?"

Fortunately, the movie was starting and Amy didn't have to answer. The girls slipped into the last row and settled down to watch.

It was a seriously stupid movie. Still, Amy and Aly and Karen were in such silly moods that it didn't matter, and they laughed uproariously at the rubber-faced actor falling all over the place.

After the movie, they found Tasha outside. "I left early," Tasha told them. "That was terrible."

Aly and Karen were still giggling. "Are you crazy?" Aly shrieked. "It was great!"

Amy gave Tasha a "What can I say?" half-smile, noncommittally mumbled something like "Yeah, well, y'know," and shrugged helplessly.

Tasha just stared straight ahead. "I need to get home," she said.

"My dad's picking us up, he'll give you guys a ride," Aly announced. Mr. Kendricks was waiting for them at the appointed place. Standing outside the car with a big, jolly grin on his face, he looked even more like he should be wearing a red suit and calling out "Ho, ho, ho."

He gave an exaggerated cry of surprise as they approached. "Oh my! Who are these beauty queens? Have any of you seen my twelve-year-old daughter?"

Amy had almost forgotten that they were still wearing the elaborate makeup. "Hi, Mr. Kendricks. This is my friend Tasha."

"Hello, Tasha. Well, what do you think of those two?" he asked, gesturing toward Amy and Aly. "Pretty amazing, huh?"

"Amazing," Tasha repeated with absolutely no enthusiasm at all. Aly opened the back door of the car.

"Dad, there are boxes in here."

"Oh, I need to put those in the trunk." Mr. Kendricks went to the rear of the car and opened it. Meanwhile, Amy lifted out one of the boxes and brought it around to him. Aly reached in and got the other box.

"Oof! What have you got in here, Dad? Bricks?"

"New tiles for the kitchen," Mr. Kendricks told her.

"And stop whining! Your twin over here didn't have any problem carrying her box, and they're exactly the same." He beamed at Amy, and Amy smiled uneasily in return. She hadn't realized how heavy the box had been.

When they reached her house, Amy saw her mother's car pulling into the driveway. Nancy got out with Dr. Hopkins, and Mr. Kendricks waved to them. The girls said their goodbyes, Amy vowing to speak to Aly on the phone later that evening, and she and Tasha got out.

Nancy had been smiling as she waved at Mr. Kendricks, but the smile disappeared when she got a good look at Amy's face. "Don't tell me you were walking around the mall like that!"

"We were just fooling around," Amy said quickly. "Hi, Dr. Hopkins. Tasha, come up to my room."

Tasha followed her up the stairs. "Amy, did you really like that movie?"

"Not particularly," Amy admitted.

"Then why were you laughing so hard? I could hear you guys before I walked out!"

"Aly liked it, so . . . you know."

"So you had to pretend you liked it too?"

Amy faced her. "What's the matter with you? Don't you like Aly?"

"She's okay, I guess. I mean, she's who she is. You're the one who's acting weird."

Amy put her hands on her hips. "What's that supposed to mean?" she demanded.

Tasha didn't flinch at her tone. "You hate wearing gobs of makeup! And you know it's wrong to sneak into a movie without paying! And you *hate* stupid movies like that! You're just faking it so you can be like Aly!"

"Oh, really?" Amy shot back. "That's a pretty strange comment, coming from you!"

Now it was Tasha's turn to ask, "What do you mean by that?"

Amy batted her eyelashes and struck a pose. " 'Oh, Dwayne, I just love aliens and mummies and you're so brave and smart.' "

"Yeah, well, what about you? 'Golly gee, Aly, we're exactly alike, I can't do simple addition either!' "

The two girls glared at each other. Then Amy gave an unusually loud yawn. "I'm tired, and I've got homework to do. I'll see you in the morning."

Tasha shook her head. "I'm going to school early—I've got a meeting. And don't wait for Eric, he's going early too. He's got a meeting with Lauren."

"Again?"

"Oh, I don't think it's so bad for him," Tasha said pointedly. "Lauren's swell." She turned and went back down the stairs. Amy followed her.

"Well, I'll see you at school tomorrow," she said.

Tasha nodded and left. Amy watched her walk across the lawn to her house and tried not to feel bad about the words they'd just exchanged. They'd had fights before; they'd get over this one.

She went into the kitchen, where her mother was fixing dinner and Dr. Hopkins was talking about a new job he'd accepted as chief of the emergency room at Westside Hospital. He claimed it was a great opportunity, but Amy suspected he wanted to be closer to Parkside and Nancy.

"I think I've lost about five pounds in the past week," Dr. Hopkins was saying. "It's not as dramatic as those TV shows, but you definitely keep moving." He turned to Amy. "I see you and Aly are getting to be pretty close friends."

"I like her a lot," Amy admitted.

"But you haven't said anything to her about—"

"No, of course not," Amy said.

"That was nice of Mr. Kendricks to drive you girls home," her mother said. "It's so out of his way."

"He looked sort of familiar to me," Dr. Hopkins remarked.

Amy grinned. "That's because he looks like Santa Claus. What time is it?"

When Nancy told her, Amy did some rapid mental calculations. "Aly should be home by now," she said. "I'm going to call her."

"You just left her!" Nancy said. "What could you possibly have to talk about?"

Amy rolled her eyes. Mothers never seemed to understand stuff like that.

ten 10

Amy dawdled over breakfast in the morning. Her mother was on the phone with Dr. Hopkins, and without much effort Amy could hear his end of the conversation almost as easily as she could hear Nancy's.

"I'm wiped out," Dr. Hopkins was saying. "Two gunshot wounds, three stabbings, and an entire bowling team with food poisoning. All before midnight."

"That's rough," Nancy sympathized.

"And that wasn't the end of it; the worst was yet to come. Four teenagers in a car wreck. The driver had been drinking, and they plowed right into a bus."

"Ohmigod," Nancy gasped. "Were there fatalities?"

"Almost," the doctor said grimly. "We barely managed to save them. One kid needed six pints of blood."

This was getting too gruesome for Amy. She shut out the voices and thought about the advice Aly had given her on the phone last night. Amy had told her about Eric's spending more and more time with the beautiful Lauren Marino, and Aly had advised her to start playing hard to get. But Amy had barely seen him at all lately—and how could a person play hard to get if the other person wasn't around to *see* her playing hard to get?

Nancy hung up the phone. "Amy, look at the time!"

"I'm leaving right now." Amy gulped down the last of her toast, grabbed her books, and took off. Glancing at her watch, she saw that she hadn't given herself the usual amount of time to walk to school. She didn't have to be late, of course. If she moved through back streets, where she was less likely to be seen, she could put on some real speed and be there in a third of the time she usually took with Tasha and Eric.

But she didn't feel like using her abilities. She ambled along at a normal, ordinary pace. And as a result, when she entered Parkside Middle School, the final bell had already rung and the halls were silent.

Her homeroom teacher looked at her in surprise and disapproval when she walked in. "Amy, you're late! Do you have an excuse?"

"No," Amy said, taking her seat. "I guess I overslept."

The teacher frowned. "That's not like you. I'm afraid I'll have to give you a demerit."

Amy didn't mind. Other kids got demerits all the time. Aly probably had zillions of them.

Later, in geography, Mr. Deadly Boring asked her to name the major exports of Paraguay. For once, she didn't know the answer to a question. She wasn't faking it either. She just hadn't read the assignment.

It would only have taken her about five minutes to do it, but she hadn't opened a textbook over the weekend. And even a photographic memory couldn't remember something that had never been seen in the first place. Mr. Deadly Boring was astonished, and her classmates were floored. Amy enjoyed every minute and decided it really wasn't very difficult to be less than perfect.

And she had another pleasurable moment after school, at her piano lesson, when Mr. Lerner told her that her playing was sloppy and full of careless errors. She hadn't been trying to make mistakes—they'd come naturally, because she hadn't bothered to practice or even glance at the sheet music since her last lesson. It was absolutely wonderful to realize that she could be so bad without any effort at all.

But she was still a superior person, of course, so she had no problem hearing Eric call to her from his bedroom window as she started up her walk that afternoon. She looked up at him, and he motioned for her to come in. She debated whether or not to agree and decided to go meet him. It would give her a chance to play hard to get.

She found both Eric and Tasha in Eric's room, huddled over his desk. "Eric's computer broke down," Tasha announced.

"It's not a big thing," Eric reported. "It's happened before. But if I take it to the repair place, I won't get it back for three days, and I have to work on the Spanish assignment."

Amy drew closer, and Eric pointed out the problem. "There's a little screw in there, and it's loose. But I can't see it, it's too dark in there."

"I was telling Eric you'd be able to see it with no problem and tighten it for him," Tasha said.

Once again, Amy was supposed to come to their rescue. Eric was depending on her extraordinary skills to save the day for him. Well, he'd have to find himself another clone.

"I'm sorry, Eric. But I've decided I don't want to use my special talents anymore."

He looked at her blankly. "What?"

"I'm trying to be more normal," she explained. "Just because I can do things other people can't do doesn't mean I have to do them all the time."

"Amy, you're not making any sense," Tasha said.

"I just want to start living like an ordinary person," Amy declared.

Eric was completely bewildered. "Why?"

Amy sauntered toward the door. "Maybe this way I'll find out who my real friends are. When I can't do them favors anymore." She didn't bother to turn around to see his reaction. It was more fun just imaging it. But she couldn't resist making one more comment before leaving the room. "Why don't you ask Lauren Marino to help you?"

Back home, she ran up to her room and went directly to her computer. Logging on, she composed an e-mail.

I just played hard to get with Eric. It was so cool, he didn't know what hit him!

Are you off from school Wednesday for the California Teachers' Conference? Do you want to come over and spend the night with me?

She sent the e-mail to Aly, and then she flopped down on her bed to read a magazine. She could always do her homework later. Or maybe not.

eleven

Amy knew her own bedroom was nowhere near as fabulous as Aly's, but Aly was nice enough to act impressed. "Very cool," she said with approval as she surveyed the room. Her eyes settled on the tall bookcase. "Have you read all those books?"

"Sure," Amy said. "Some of them more than once. Like *Charlotte's Web*. I got it when I was eight, and I still like to read it once in a while. It's my all-time favorite book. Does it make you cry too?"

"I've never read it," Aly told her.

Amy was shocked. "I'll lend you my copy. Or I'll buy you one of your own for your birthday."

"I'm not much of a reader," Aly said.

Amy remembered not having seen any books in Aly's room when she spent the night. "You don't like books?"

"I'm not any better at reading than I am at math," Aly admitted with an abashed grin.

"Oh." Amy shrugged that off. She didn't care about their differences; she preferred to think about what they had in common. "Well, it's not like we're going to be reading tonight. I've got some great videos."

Aly looked around again. "Where's your TV?"

"I don't have my own," Amy had to admit. "We'll have to watch in the living room. But my mother won't bug us. She's got a meeting at the university tomorrow at eight in the morning, so she'll go to bed early. We can make popcorn and brownies and order pizzas. Or we can have Chinese food delivered. Do you like Chinese food?"

Aly's eyes began to sparkle in a way that was becoming familiar to Amy. "I've actually got a better idea."

"What?" Amy hoped Aly wasn't going to suggest that they order sushi. She'd never developed much of a taste for raw fish.

"Let's go to an underground rave."

"A what?"

"A rave! It's an all-night dance party in a secret place."

Amy had heard of raves. She just hadn't expected to

hear about a rave tonight. No one she knew had ever been to one. "Do you go to raves?"

"No," Aly confessed. "But Karen's sister, Kristin, is seventeen and goes to them all the time. Their parents are out of town so Kristin's taking Karen with her tonight, and she said we could come too."

Amy was doubtful. "Don't you have to be eighteen to get in?"

"Are you kidding? Anyone can get in. The secret is knowing where it's going to be, and Kristin gave me the address." She pulled a crumpled paper out of her pocket and showed it to Amy. The street name seemed vaguely familiar.

"Isn't that in West Hollywood?"

"Yeah, I think so. We'll have to hitchhike."

Amy winced. Hitchhiking was an activity that had always been expressly forbidden to her.

Aly didn't notice her reaction. "As soon as your mother goes to sleep, we'll sneak out, and we can be back before she gets up in the morning."

"It's not going to be that easy," Amy told her. "My mother's got ears in the back of her head. If I get up in the middle of the night for water, even if she's sound asleep, she almost always hears me. Her hearing's incredible, it's almost as good as—" She caught herself. "Well, as good as someone who . . . who has really good hearing. Anyway, she'll catch us before we can get down the stairs."

Aly's face fell. "And there's no other way we can get out of the house?"

She looked so disappointed that Amy started to feel disappointed too. Suddenly an evening of videos and popcorn seemed awfully lame. Amy's eyes moved to the window by her bed. Aly followed her glance and read her mind.

"Have you ever climbed out of it before?"

"Once," Amy admitted. "There's a tree . . ." They went to the window and peered out. A thick, strong-looking branch extended out toward the window, and there were solid branches all the way down.

Aly brightened. "I used to climb trees all the time when I was a kid. Let's do it! How many chances do you get to go to a real rave?"

Amy doubted another opportunity would be coming along anytime soon. From what she'd heard, a rave was mostly about dancing, and as long as they stayed away from drugs and alcohol, she and Aly would be okay.

She didn't think it was going to be very difficult to sneak out of the house. Nancy wouldn't suspect; it would never occur to her that Amy might try something like this. Amy tried not to feel guilty, and she kept telling herself that what her mother didn't know—and would *never* know—couldn't hurt her. And the idea of another normal, typical teen adventure with Aly was very enticing.

Amy psyched herself up and was ready to take off as soon as Nancy went to bed at ten o'clock. "Let's give her ten minutes to fall asleep before we leave," she told Aly.

Aly agreed. "There's something we need to do first anyway." She opened her overnight bag and pulled out a sack. "Check this out." The sack was full of tiny containers of cosmetics.

"Where did you get all this stuff?"

"It's from Karen's mother. Are you any good at putting on makeup?"

"Not really," Amy admitted. She rarely wore anything more than a little gloss once in a while. Tasha had been right about that—Amy hated the feeling of globs of cosmetics on her face. "Do we have to wear this stuff?"

"It'll make us look a lot older," Aly said.

"I thought you said they'll let anyone into a rave."

"They will," Aly assured her. "But the other kids there are going to be a lot older, and if we want any guys to dance with us, we'd better not look too young."

Aly wasn't any better at applying the makeup than Amy was. By the time they finished, Amy thought they both looked more like clowns than sophisticated older teens. But she presumed the lights would be low, and it wasn't as if she was going to run into anyone from Parkside.

"Should we dress up?" she wondered.

"I wish we could," Aly said. "But I don't think we're going to make it down and up that tree in short skirts and heels. Let's just wear jeans. I brought us something special to wear with them." And from her bag she produced two identical red glitter T-shirts. That was enough for Amy to feel like a completely different person.

She opened the window. "Should I go first?"

Aly nodded. "I'll watch how you do it."

Amy perched on the windowsill with her legs dangling and hoped that neither Tasha nor Eric happened to be looking out their windows at the moment. Taking a deep breath, she lunged toward the limb that extended closest to the window. Grasping it, she swung her legs around till they settled on a lower branch. She could have jumped from there and landed on her feet, but she didn't want Aly to try that. So she edged down, limb by limb, until she hit the ground.

Looking up, she saw Aly sitting on the ledge, preparing to take her leap. Then Amy noticed something she should have realized earlier. The limb wasn't all that close to the window. She had been able to cover the distance with her unusual ability to stretch, but a person with a body that operated in the normal way wouldn't be able to do it.

She didn't know what to do. If she shrieked out a warning, it would wake her mother. If she didn't—

It was too late. Aly was off the ledge, and she wasn't going to make it.

In less than a tenth of a second, Amy was scrambling up the tree. She managed to intercede just as Aly was making her impossible reach for the limb. Grabbing her around the waist, Amy used one arm to drop from limb to limb until they reached the ground.

"Ohmigod," Aly gasped.

"Shhh, you'll wake up the whole neighborhood," Amy whispered, shooting a worried glance up at the window. She gave Aly a moment to catch her breath. She actually needed that moment herself, too.

"I can't believe I'm such a wimp," Aly moaned.

Amy tried to make her feel better. "That branch is farther from the window than it looks," she said.

Aly gazed up toward the top of the tree. "I don't get it. You're no bigger than I am. How come you could reach the limb and I couldn't?"

"I guess I'm in pretty good shape," Amy suggested lamely.

"I'm going to start working out," Aly declared. "If you can reach that branch, I should be able to do it too.

And how did you get down? I know you're strong, but I weigh the same as you. How did you carry me?"

"I was leaning against the tree, so it's not like I was bearing all your weight." Amy knew she was talking nonsense in her effort to explain what she'd done, and she had to get Aly to stop asking questions. "Come on. If we're gonna go, let's go."

She was more than a little nervous about hitch-hiking. She'd read the articles in teen magazines warning of the dangers, and she knew there were crazy people out there who might pick them up with evil intentions. But as it turned out, they were in luck—even though it didn't seem so at the moment. As they were standing on the street with their thumbs out, a police car pulled up.

The uniformed officer looked at them sternly. "What are you kids doing?"

Aly spoke quickly. "We're trying to get home," she said. "We took the wrong bus and now we're lost. And we couldn't call our parents because their phone is out of order."

"Then you should have called the police," he scolded them. "Do you have any idea how dangerous hitch-hiking can be? Get in the car, I'll take you home. Where do you live?"

Aly gave him an address, and he took off. Along the

way, he continued to lecture them, frightening them with truly awful stories of kids who had been kidnapped or seriously hurt by hitchhikers. By the time they reached the street in West Hollywood where the rave was being held, Amy was convinced they had taken their lives in their hands. She had no idea how they were going to get back to her house, but she knew it wouldn't be by hitchhiking.

Aly indicated an apartment complex looming ahead of them. "It's right there, where we live. You can just let us off on the street."

The policeman snorted. "What do you think this is, a taxi? I'm taking you two right to your door and handing you over to your parents."

The girls looked at each other in despair. Even Aly seemed at a loss for words. But at that moment they had a *real* stroke of luck. They heard a crackling over the car radio and then a voice came on.

"All cars in the vicinity of Longwood, proceed directly to four-six-one, armed robbery in progress."

"You kids get out," the cop barked, and they were happy to do so. The police car sped out of sight.

Aly grinned. "We owe that burglar a great big thank-you." She grabbed Amy's hand, and they ran across the wide street. "That must be where the rave is," she said, pointing.

Amy looked. "Where? All I see is a parking garage."

But that was exactly where the party was going on—at the bottom level of an underground parking garage. They didn't have the special code to take the elevator, so they had to climb down about a thousand steps till they reached a heavy metal door. Aly pulled it open.

Amy had never heard music so loud in her life. Thumping, tuneless techno sounds seemed to be shaking the entire structure—or at least her entire body. She felt like she was vibrating. There were so many people moving to the same beat that they seemed like one throbbing mass of humanity. Streaks of multicolored lights cut into the darkness, adding to the unreal ambiance of the place.

This time it was Amy who took Aly's hand. "Let's stay together," she said.

"Absolutely," Aly replied. And they thrust themselves into the throng.

twelve 12

Immediately they were caught up in the music and the feverish excitement. People were bumping and crashing into each other. Amy kept hold of Aly's hand. They didn't want to be separated, so they danced together, and Amy found herself getting into the frenzied spirit, the sense of total abandon. She could see that Aly was into it too—her dancing was positively wild. Amy had to work at keeping up with her, but she was enjoying every minute of it. With their identical looks and identical glitter T-shirts, they got some admiring looks, and for once Amy didn't mind the attention. Because it wasn't directed at her alone, at her as some kind of freak. For once she felt like she actually belonged.

"Do you see Karen?" Aly yelled. Amy wasn't sure if she was actually hearing Aly over the din or just reading her lips.

"No, not yet," she yelled back.

"What?"

Reminding herself that Aly didn't have her hearing or lipreading ability, she responded by shaking her head, and she didn't miss a beat in the process. The rave must have had a professional DJ, because there was never a pause in the music. She estimated that they had been dancing for more than half an hour, and she could have gone on a lot longer. But Aly was only human. Amy could tell she needed a break. She pointed to the door, and Aly nodded. Together they pushed their way through the pulsating mob and finally reached the metal door. Just outside, the elevator door opened and more people poured out of it. Aly and Amy jumped in and rode up to the ground level.

They burst out onto the top open deck of the parking garage and took big gulps of not-exactly-fresh air. A bunch of teens were leaning against a car smoking, and the acrid smell saturated the area. But not even that could dampen the girls' spirits.

Aly pointed at Amy. "Girlfriend, you can *dance*!"

Amy was pleased to hear that. "Really?"

"You have to teach me some of those moves."

"Okay, sure," Amy said, and wondered if that was possible. She'd picked them up automatically, just watching other dancers. It was just one more genetic benefit.

"Aly! Amy!"

"I hear Karen," Amy told her.

"I don't," Aly responded. "What do you have, some kind of sixth sense?"

"Here she comes now," Amy said, pointing.

Aly looked in the same direction. "Where? You're seeing things!" But a moment later, Karen was by their side.

"Isn't this awesome!" Karen exclaimed. "I've been dancing all night. I am *so* wiped out, I can barely stand up!"

"Where's your sister?" Aly asked.

Karen gestured. "Over there, with some very cute boys. Come on!"

Kristin turned out to be a glamorous version of Karen. The boys she was with were more like men. There were three of them. One had about a dozen tattoos all over his arms, another had pink streaks in yellow hair, and the third looked boringly ordinary. But he was the one who seemed most impressed with the newcomers.

"Wow! Twins!"

"Kristin, this is Amy, I told you about her," Karen said.

"Hi, Amy," Kristin drawled. She wasn't standing all that close to Amy, but Amy's sense of smell was as sharp as her vision and her hearing. She could tell that Kristin had been drinking something alcoholic.

"Let's get out of here," the tattooed guy said. "I know a better party." Amy found herself hustled along to a nearby car.

"We can't all fit in there!" she protested.

But somehow they did. The ordinary guy got into the driver's seat, while Pink Streak sat in the passenger seat with Kristin on his lap. In the backseat, the tattooed guy pulled Aly onto his lap, and Amy and Karen squeezed in next to him. Karen barely had time to get the back door closed before they sped off, accompanied by the screech of burning rubber.

It was then, with all the doors closed, that Amy got the full impact of the odor—and she realized all the older kids had been drinking. The way the driver swerved onto the main road confirmed this.

"I don't think that guy should be driving," she whispered to Aly, but Aly was giggling about something the boy under her was whispering in her ear.

No one else seemed to notice how drunk the driver was. Karen had her head on Amy's shoulder, and she appeared to be half asleep. In the passenger seat, Kristin and Pink Streak were all over each other.

There was a jolt as the car jumped the curb. The driver got it back onto the road, but then he had to swerve hard to avoid a truck. Karen was knocked against the door, and suddenly she was fully awake. She grabbed Amy's hand.

"What's going on?" she asked, clearly frightened.

And now Aly was aware of the situation. "Tell your friend to pull over," she said to the owner of the lap she was sitting on. He just laughed.

"Kristin!" Karen wailed as the driver ran a red light. "Make him stop!"

But Kristin was now trying to make someone else stop doing something. Pink Streak was attempting to get more romantic than Kristin wanted him to be. "No! Don't do that!" Her words were slurred but completely audible. The boy wasn't paying any attention to them. It was at that point Amy realized she couldn't let them go on like this.

"Can you let us out, please?" she asked the driver.

He didn't seem to hear her. She repeated the request with even more urgency.

"We're almost there," the guy told her. But she had a sick feeling that it didn't matter how close they were—because they weren't going to make it.

"I want to drive," she said suddenly.

"Yeah, right," the guy snickered. "Like I'm going to let you."

Like you're going to be able to stop me, Amy thought. She didn't bother to say it; she just went into action. The boy had no idea he was dealing with someone who could do what ordinary people couldn't.

In less than a fraction of a second, she managed to get herself up onto the back of the driver's seat. With one firm push, she had shoved the driver over on top of Kristin and her seatmate and had taken his place at the wheel.

She'd never driven before in her life. She'd never even had a lesson. But she'd sat in the passenger seat next to her mother so many times that she immediately recollected the necessary actions and knew exactly what to do. Clutching the steering wheel tightly, she checked in the rearview mirror to make sure no one was too close behind her in the next lane. With a shrug of her right shoulder, she thrust off the efforts of the boy to regain control of the wheel and gently applied pressure to the brake as she steered the car over to the side of the road.

As soon as the car stopped, Aly got her back door open and jumped out. Karen jumped over the tattooed guy and scrambled out after her. The tattooed guy followed. "Hey, where are you going?" he protested. Meanwhile, Amy had run around to the passenger side of the front seat and opened the door. Kristin had recovered sufficiently to get herself out of the car. Amy pulled out the driver and Pink Streak.

"Whaddya think yer doin'?" the driver shrieked at Amy. He made a gesture like he was going to hit her, but she ducked his fist easily and he tripped. Pink Streak hadn't given up on Kristin—he lunged at her and pushed her to the ground. Amy rushed over and with one hand pulled his face up high enough so she could slug him with the other hand. He went out like a light.

But the other two guys were still conscious, and they weren't happy. Fortunately, whatever they'd been drinking was making them move slowly.

"Get back in the car," Amy yelled at the girls, and they obeyed. She ran back around to the driver's seat. The car's owner was right behind her, but there was no way he could match her speed. She was in the seat with the door locked before he could make his way around the car, and with one quick look over her shoulder, she hit the gas.

Beside her, in the passenger seat, Kristin was crying. In the backseat, Karen and Aly were cheering. "Ay-*mee*! Ay-*mee*! Ay-*mee*!"

Aly leaned over Amy's shoulder. "You are so *incredible*!" she proclaimed. "You saved us! You are the *best*!"

Karen was just as thrilled. "Aly, why can't you do stuff like that? You're just like she is!"

"I'm sure I can, I've just never tried," Aly declared excitedly. "But I will!"

Amy was too busy visualizing a map of Los Angeles to respond to that comment. She followed the mental map toward her own neighborhood.

"I wanna go home," Kristin moaned. "Take me home."

Amy could see that there wasn't enough gas left in the tank to get the sisters home and then drive herself and Aly home too. And she didn't have enough money to get more gas. Not to mention the fact that she didn't want to draw attention to a twelve-year-old girl driving a car. So she concentrated on getting them all to her own house. Kristin and Karen could stay on the sofa—but how was Amy going to explain their presence to her mother in the morning?

She was pondering this question as she pulled up in front of her house. The girls got out of the car. Aly and Karen were still screaming about how wonderful Amy had been.

"Those guys didn't know what hit them!" Karen was squealing. "And you saved my sister from that creep!"

"Shhh!" Amy hissed urgently. "Be quiet!"

But it was too late. Over at the Morgan house, an upstairs light went on. A second later she could see Tasha's face at the window.

Amy stood there, frozen. Now what was she supposed to do? If they went in through the door, Nancy was bound to hear them. But there was no way Kristin could make it up the tree in her condition. And now here was Tasha, in her bathrobe and slippers, coming out of her house.

"Amy, what's going on?"

At least Tasha was discreet enough to keep her voice down. Quickly and quietly Amy summarized the evening's events. Happily, Tasha realized this wasn't the time or place to begin any lectures on conduct. She even came up with a possible solution.

Nodding toward Karen and Kristin, she said, "I'll go call a taxi to take them home."

"I don't think we have enough money for a taxi," Karen told her. Amy knew she didn't either. Aly checked her wallet, but she had very little cash.

Once again Tasha came to the rescue. "I've got some money, I'll lend it to you."

She went back into the house and returned in a moment. "Here's the money, and I called the taxi. It should be here any minute."

And it was. Karen pushed her semiconscious sister in

and gave the driver their address. Amy and Aly thanked Tasha profusely, and Amy promised to call the next day. Tasha went back into her house, and Amy and Aly climbed the tree.

When they were safe and sound in Amy's bedroom, Aly collapsed on Amy's twin bed. "Wait here," Amy whispered. She went out into the hall and pressed her ear against her mother's bedroom door. She could hear Nancy's calm, even breathing.

Back in her room, she fell onto her own bed and looked at Aly. Without even speaking, the two of them covered their identical mouths and burst into muffled laughter.

"What a night!" Aly gasped.

Amy had no difficulty agreeing. "This is going to get two full pages in my journal!"

They spent the next twenty minutes going over every detail of their wild evening. And when they finished, they both acknowledged that they were starving.

Amy crept downstairs and gathered tortilla chips, salsa, and a pint of ice cream. Back in her room, the girls pigged out and continued to relive the experience.

"You know what's really exciting?" Aly said. "Knowing we can take care of ourselves like that! I mean, those guys were *big*!"

Amy agreed, but something about Aly's reaction

bothered her. And Aly's next words made real fear shoot through her.

"I won't ever have to be afraid of anyone anymore! Just teach me how you did all that, okay?"

Amy winced. How could she tell Aly that there was no way she could teach her to do what she had done? No way, nohow.

thirteen 13

At their usual table in the school cafeteria, Amy pushed an envelope across the table toward Tasha. "Here's the money Karen and her sister owe you for the taxi. Sorry it took so long to get it, but I just saw Karen again yesterday at Aly's."

It had been almost a week since that fateful night, and Tasha had been kind enough not to mention it. "Thanks," she said, putting the envelope in her bag. "What did you and Aly do this weekend?"

"We hung out at her place," Amy told her. "On Saturday we went bowling."

"I haven't been bowling in ages," Tasha commented. "Was it fun?"

Amy nodded. Then she sighed. "I was trying not to knock all the pins down, which was fairly easy. Then Aly got really competitive, so I had to work twice as hard to get the ball into the gutter so I wouldn't win."

"At least you were doing something safe," Tasha said. "I still can't believe you went to a rave. And that you got into a car with strange guys! Amy, I hate to sound like one of our mothers, but that could have been really dangerous for all of you."

Amy shrugged. "We ended up okay."

"Because *you* took care of everything," Tasha pointed out. "What would they have done if you hadn't been there?" She frowned. "And I thought you told me you weren't going to use your powers anymore."

Amy flushed. "I didn't want to. But I sort of had to. Look, I'm tired of talking about it. What did *you* do this weekend?"

"I went back to the carnival with Dwayne. And I did something stupid."

"What?"

"Well, there was this special booth that was set up like a quiz show. Sort of like *Jeopardy!* Dwayne and I played it, and the category was state capitals."

Amy knew what was coming. Back in fourth grade,

Tasha had been the first in their class to have all the capitals memorized. "And you beat him," she said.

Tasha nodded.

"See?" Amy said. "You can't hide your smarts from him all the time."

"Just like you can't hide your powers from Aly," Tasha replied.

Amy drummed her fingers on the table and changed the subject again. "Is Eric still having meetings with Lauren?"

"Yeah, his Spanish assignment is due tomorrow. I think he's feeling pretty good about it, though. She's helped him a lot."

Amy smiled thinly and wondered if Lauren was still going to "help" him once the assignment was finished.

"Do you have piano after school today?" Tasha asked.

Amy hesitated. "Sort of."

"What do you mean, 'sort of'? Either you have it or you don't."

"Yeah, I've got piano. Hey, I'll give you my cupcake for your apple." Amy would have given Tasha anything to distract her. She knew Tasha wouldn't approve of the plan she and Aly had come up with—the plan she put into action as soon as school let out.

When the last class period ended, Amy headed directly for the bus stop and started on the long trip to the Hillcrest Recreation Center. This time she had to wait longer between each bus transfer, but that was fine, since Aly's class didn't start until four-thirty. She still got there in plenty of time.

She didn't have to show the membership ID that Aly had lent to her. The busy receptionist recognized her—or thought she did—and waved her right in.

Two other girls were already in the dressing room, changing clothes and putting on their skates. "Hi, Aly," they chorused. Amy smiled and nodded. She didn't know their names, but she and Aly had concocted a way to deal with this kind of situation. She pointed to her throat and mouthed the words "Can't talk."

"Laryngitis, huh?" one of the girls said sympathetically. "I had that before; it's awful. Why didn't you use it for an excuse to stay home? You hate this class."

Amy responded to this with a smile and a shrug.

Amy had ice-skated before, but only a couple of times and just for fun. She didn't know the names of the different moves, but she knew she would be able to do them. All she needed was a single demonstration of a spin or a jump and she'd be able to do a perfect imitation. Amy just hoped Aly wasn't having too much difficulty with the dreary piano teacher.

She snapped to attention as Donna, the ice-skating teacher, called on each of the girls to do something called an axel jump. Amy watched the skaters struggle through it, but she didn't think it looked too hard. Then Donna said they were going to learn a new back spin—but she had never called on Aly/Amy to do the axel.

"Excuse me," Amy said. "You forgot me."

"Aly!" one of her classmates exclaimed. "Your laryngitis is gone!"

Amy gulped. For someone with superior intelligence, she could be pretty dumb sometimes. "Uh, yeah. I guess so. Funny how it cleared up just like that." She turned to the teacher. "Should I do the axel now?"

Donna smiled kindly. "I don't think you're ready for this yet, Aly. You remember what happened when you tried last week."

Of course, Amy didn't remember, but she figured Aly had messed up big-time. Still, it annoyed her the way the teacher just assumed Aly couldn't have gotten any better. Aly had told her that Donna was always picking on her and pointing out that she was the worst in the group. Amy would show her. "I've been practicing," she declared. And before the teacher could say anything more, she began to skate. Building momentum, she jumped and did not one but two turns in the air.

There was a moment of dead silence when she

finished. Then her classmates cheered, and Donna looked totally incredulous. "Aly! That's amazing!" she said, and she seemed honestly pleased. That was when it hit Amy that maybe she had just done something very stupid.

When the session ended, the other girls and Donna left and free skate time on the ice began. There were only a few solitary skaters, and Amy went over to the viewers' section to sit and wait. Just a few minutes later she saw Aly come in and skate toward her.

"How was piano?" Amy wanted to know.

"Awful!" Aly said, but she was laughing. "Your creepy teacher says you're getting worse. In fact, he's going to recommend to your mother that you consider a different instrument."

Amy clapped her hands in delight. "That's fantastic!"

"How did *I* do in skating today?" Aly asked.

Amy bit her lower lip. "Well . . . pretty good, actually. You did a double axel."

Aly was stunned. "What? A double axel? Amy, I can't do a *single* axel! I can't even get in the air!" Then she grinned. "I'll bet Donna was impressed."

"Oh, she was," Amy assured her. "But now I'm wondering . . . what are you going to do next week when she expects you to do it again?"

Aly's response was immediate. "I'll do it again. Look,

if you can do it, I can do it. I just need to practice. Come on, show me how it's done."

Maybe, with a lot of practice, Aly *would* be able to do an axel. Amy followed Aly onto the ice and demonstrated the jump. "That doesn't look so hard," Aly said, but her voice was uncertain. And when she attempted the jump, she fell flat on her face.

"Are you okay?" Amy asked anxiously.

"Of course I'm okay. I just skidded, that's all. I'll start over." But Aly's second effort was no better. Nor was her third or her fourth. As she had told Amy, she couldn't even get off the ice.

"I just don't understand," she wailed. "Are you sure you've never had any skating lessons?"

Amy felt awful. "Yes, I'm sure."

"Then how did you do that double axel?"

"I don't know," Amy lied. "I guess maybe it comes naturally."

"That doesn't make any sense," Aly fumed. "How can it come naturally to you and not to me?"

Amy could only lie again and tell Aly she had absolutely no explanation. Fortunately, she didn't have to continue the charade. Mrs. Kendricks had arrived to pick them up.

The girls went back to the dressing room to change

and take off their skates. Aly didn't say much. She still looked confused and unhappy.

Mrs. Kendricks greeted them with a big smile. "You know, I honestly don't think I can tell you two apart! It's like that movie *The Parent Trap.* Now I understand how those twins could fool their own mother and father. I really do believe you two had to have been sisters separated at birth."

"I guess we'll never know for sure," Amy said.

fourteen 14

Nancy Candler wasn't happy about Amy's request. "You want to sleep over at Aly's again tonight?"

"It's Friday, Mom. No school tomorrow, remember?"

"That's not the point, Amy. It's just that you two have been spending so much time together."

"So what?"

"Amy, we've talked about this before. I'm worried about you girls becoming too close. I just don't think it can be a very healthy relationship. For either of you."

Amy knew it wouldn't do her any good to let her irritation show at this point, not if she wanted to get out of the house anytime soon. Still, it was hard to keep her voice even. "Mom, we're not in any danger. Nobody's been watching us, no one's tried to kidnap us, and Aly still doesn't know anything about Project Crescent."

But that didn't assuage her mother's concern. "But you have to be very careful, Amy, and not just to protect yourself. It's not just the organization that I'm worried about. You don't want to hurt Aly."

"Aly's my friend. Why would I hurt her?"

Nancy sighed wearily. "I'm not saying you'd hurt her intentionally. But you have to be realistic. It might be easy for you to pretend you're just like she is. But it would be very dangerous for her to think she can be like you."

Amy was glad she hadn't slipped and told her mother how she and Aly had switched lessons. So Aly couldn't do a double axel—big deal. She'd get over it. But in the back of her mind, Amy knew that wasn't the real issue.

At least she wasn't forbidden to spend the night at Aly's. Nancy even drove her there. "Tell Aly's mother I'm sorry I can't come in to say hello." She was meeting Dr. Hopkins for a quick dinner at the hospital cafeteria. "The poor man is on duty all night," she said. "He can only take twenty minutes off for dinner, so if I'm not there on time, I won't see him at all."

Amy was curious. "Does Dr. Hopkins think I spend too much time with Aly?"

Nancy couldn't help smiling. "He thinks I worry too much and that you've got more good sense than I give you credit for."

Amy grinned. "I think you should marry Dr. Hopkins, Mom."

"Get out of the car," her mother ordered, but Amy didn't miss the pink in her cheeks. "Have fun, and don't get into any trouble. Use the good sense that David thinks you have."

It was a good thing her mother hadn't been able to stop to say hello to Mrs. Kendricks. Aly's parents and little brother weren't home.

"They went out to the airport to meet my uncle," Aly told Amy. "He has a three-hour layover there. I told Mom your mother wouldn't mind if they weren't here."

Amy wasn't so sure that was true, but what her mother didn't know wouldn't hurt her. She showed Aly her bag of videos. "I brought *Scream 1* and *Scream 2*. So we can scream all night."

"I've got a better idea," Aly announced. Her eyes were the brightest Amy had ever seen. "Let's go to the carnival."

Amy had almost become accustomed to Aly's sudden

plans, but she was never fully prepared. "The carnival?" she repeated.

"This is the last day. It'll be a whole year before we can get another dose of cotton candy."

An evening at the carnival certainly had the potential for more fun than an evening of watching videos. "But how are we going to get there?"

An extra sparkle lit Aly's eyes. "We'll drive!"

Amy gulped. "Drive?" she echoed.

"Sure! My mother's car is here, and they won't be back from the airport for at least four hours. They'll never even know."

Amy considered this. "But what if we get stopped by the police? I don't have a driver's license."

Aly shrugged. "Don't worry, I'll come up with a story. I'll say it's an emergency and you're taking me to a hospital." She rearranged her features into an expression of agony. "I'm sick, Officer. I feel like I'm going to die."

It was a pretty good act. "But what if the police follow us to the hospital? Or what if they call an ambulance?"

Aly groaned. "What if, what if, what if. What if there's an earthquake? It's not like you can plan for everything. Come on, it would be so much fun."

What was it Dr. Hopkins had said about her good

sense? Amy tried to rationalize what she knew was really a bad decision. If she didn't agree to drive, Aly might insist on driving herself to the carnival. Amy had to go with her, if only to protect her. That was using her good sense, right?

Besides, she really wanted to go. So she shoved the voices of Dr. Hopkins, her mother, and her own conscience to the back of her mind and accepted the car keys from Aly.

"I'm going to watch what you do," Aly said as she buckled her seat belt. "Maybe I can drive us home."

"It's not that easy," Amy said quickly.

"How come you know how to drive?"

Amy made up a story. She couldn't let Aly think that any twelve-year-old could drive. "My mother taught me, just in case of emergency. Because it's just her and me living together. It took days and days of lessons. Driving is *hard.*"

Aly didn't look particularly convinced, and Amy knew she might have to come up with more persuasive reasons to keep Aly from demanding to take the steering wheel on the way home. But she wasn't going to worry about that now. She was looking forward to another wild and crazy night.

Driving as carefully as possible, Amy relied on her

supersharp instincts to respond to any situation that might arise. But even so, she kept a wary eye out for police, who might find her presence behind the wheel disturbing.

"Do you ever wonder what our real mother was like?" Aly asked.

Amy was glad she had the road to focus on. She didn't want to look at Aly while discussing this subject. "I've never really thought about it," she said carefully.

"It must have been hard on her to give us up for adoption," Aly mused. "She must have been really young. Or maybe she was just too poor to keep us. I'll bet she wonders what happened to us. Have you ever thought about trying to find her?"

"No."

"Adopted people do that all the time, you know. There are associations that will help you find your birth parents. Most of them have Web sites. Maybe our mother is using one of those sites to find *us*. We should start searching the Internet for clues."

"Mmm." Amy kept her tone noncommittal. She knew very well that there was no poor, sad young woman searching for them. She'd have to think of some way to discourage Aly from investigating. It would be a total waste of time. But how could she convince Aly of this without telling her too much?

It was as if Aly knew that Amy was keeping something from her. "Amy . . . if we're identical twins, how come you can do things I can't do?"

"Because—because we're still different people, even if we are identical." Amy wasn't sure that made any sense, so she went on rapidly. "Like, I'm sure there are things you can do that I can't do."

"Like what?"

"Um . . . can you do a cartwheel?"

"Sure."

"Well, I can't!" Amy lied. "And—and how are you in spelling?"

"Okay," Aly replied.

"There you go!" Amy said brightly. "I'm a *terrible* speller!"

She stopped at a red light and took a quick glance at Aly. Was Aly buying all these stories, all these lies? This was the hardest friendship Amy had ever tried to maintain.

But this wasn't any ordinary friendship. The bond between them was special. And worth lying for.

She was still trying to think of a better way to handle things with Aly when she pulled into the parking area by the carnival.

"Something's wrong," she said. "There aren't any bright lights on."

"You're right," Aly cried in dismay. "It's closed!"

"I thought you said this was the last day," Amy said.

"I guess I was looking at yesterday's newspaper," Aly confessed.

Amy peered into the darkness. "They haven't packed up yet."

"How can you see in the dark?" Aly demanded.

"Um . . . I can't. I'm just guessing that the booths and stuff are there. Because . . . because I can see the Ferris wheel. But it doesn't matter, anyway, because the place is definitely closed. What do you want to do now?"

Amy looked at Aly and was alarmed to see that dangerous sparkle in her clone's eyes. What could Aly be thinking of now?

"We'll go to the carnival," Aly announced.

"Huh?"

"There's gotta be a way we can get in. Come on!" Aly jumped out of the car. Amy had no choice but to follow her.

The carnival was surrounded by a chain-link fence. They didn't bother to search for a gate, since it would surely be locked. Instead, both girls jumped onto the fence and began to climb. It wasn't easy, but it didn't require any super-powers. Amy got herself over the top first and dropped to the ground so she could break

Aly's fall. But Aly managed to scramble down on her own, and she was very pleased with herself.

"Hey, I'm not such a wimp!"

"Of course you're not," Amy said warmly. Privately she wondered if the carnival people had any idea how easy it was to break in.

Not that there was much reason for anyone to *want* to break in. As far as Amy could tell, the deserted carnival grounds offered little in the way of entertainment. The booths were closed and padlocked, the refreshment stands were bare, the rides were still. It was eerie, walking around and remembering what it had looked like when it was full of noise and light and sugary smells.

They paused when they reached the merry-go-round. Amy stepped up onto the carousel and stroked a horse with a golden mane. "I loved the merry-go-round when I was a little kid," she told Aly. "I could ride around and around for hours."

"Me too!" Aly said. "In fact, when I was here last week, I was dying to ride it. But I was too embarrassed."

Amy grinned. "It was the same for me. I kept fantasizing about jumping onto a horse and riding with all the little kids."

"There's no one here to see us now," Aly remarked.

"That's true," Amy agreed. "But there's no one here to run the merry-go-round either."

"How hard could it be?" Aly wondered aloud. She weaved in and out of the carousel horses until she reached the center pole. "I've always seen a man standing here. So the controls have to be here too." She poked around. "Yes, here they are!"

"You probably need a key or something," Amy said.

"Give me the car keys," Aly said.

Amy tossed them to her. Aly began jiggling the key in a slot. "I feel like it's activating something." A few seconds later they heard the carousel begin to play its familiar tune. And the horses began to move.

"I can't believe it!" Amy squealed. "You got it to work!"

"I'm good with my hands," Aly said proudly. "Come on, let's ride!" They each chose a horse and jumped on.

It was glorious. The tinkling music broke the dark silence and turned the place into something magical. Amy felt like a character in a fairy tale. She looked over her shoulder at Aly. Her expression was blissful, and it was clear to Amy that she was appreciating this experience in the very same way. Amy suddenly felt an enormous yearning to share everything with Aly. To tell her that they had never shared the same womb but had been cultivated in the same test tube.

But what would this knowledge do to Aly? How would it affect her to learn that she wasn't a normal human being? And that she wasn't even a successful clone? Amy couldn't predict how Aly would react. But she had a pretty strong feeling that Aly would suffer.

Now going around and around in circles was getting dull. "How do we stop this thing?" Amy asked.

"I guess we'll have to jump off," Aly said. "Because I don't think it's going to stop on its own."

In fact, the merry-go-round had picked up speed. It wasn't a problem for Amy. She swung her leg over her horse and hopped off.

She watched in alarm as Aly started to imitate her moves. "Wait," Amy called out. "I'll see if I can do something with the controls to make it slow down."

Only Aly didn't wait. She too swung her leg over her horse and hopped off. But she didn't have Amy's extraordinary balance. She fell, hard, right on her face.

Amy knelt next to her. "Are you okay?" she asked anxiously.

Aly rose slowly. "Yeah, I just got my breath knocked out." She grimaced as she brushed the dirt off her jeans. "I'm such a klutz."

She had that "I don't get it" look on her face again, and Amy began to feel uneasy. "Well, we've had our adventure," she said. "Let's go home and watch videos." She guided Aly to the edge of the carousel, and together they jumped off.

"Amy . . . why are you so much better at everything than I am?"

"Aly, come on, that's not true! I'm better at some things, but you're better than me at other things."

"My parents think you're better than I am at everything."

Amy stared at her in disbelief. "They do?"

"They say you're stronger and smarter too. They want me to be more like you."

Now Amy was feeling very uncomfortable. "How do they know—I mean, why do they think that?"

"I'm not sure," Aly said. "But they keep telling me I can learn from you. They say I should spend more time with you to figure it. They think I can be more like you."

Amy shivered. She couldn't imagine her own mother telling her to try to be like someone else. She couldn't imagine Tasha's mother telling Tasha that either. It didn't seem like a normal thing for a parent to say. "I think you're just fine the way you are," she told Aly. "Now, let's go home."

Aly was staring beyond Amy toward the Ferris wheel. "You know what would be cool? If we could ride on that by ourselves."

"And get stuck at the top?" Amy shuddered. "No thanks."

Aly didn't seem to hear her. "I'll bet I could get it to work."

"Are you nuts?" Amy exclaimed. "You saw how the merry-go-round didn't stop. At least we were only a few feet off the ground when we jumped. Can you imagine jumping off *that* thing? Do you know how fast it moves?"

"What's the matter?" Aly challenged her. "Are you scared?"

Amy thought about that. Was she scared? Not really, not for herself. But for Aly . . . "Yes," she said.

"Liar," Aly said with a grin. "Come on, let's do it." She started toward the Ferris wheel.

"Aly!"

"What?"

"We can't go on that Ferris wheel. It's way too dangerous."

Aly stared at her in a way that made Amy feel she could see right through her. "Dangerous for me, you mean. You think I can't handle it."

"It's dangerous for both of us," Amy insisted. "We're going back to the car, now."

Aly's eyes sparkled, but this time it was scary. "Who's got the car keys?" She patted her pocket and Amy heard the jangle.

"Aly!" she cried out again. But she was yelling at Aly's back. Aly was already running toward the Ferris wheel.

Amy was tempted to run after her. To use her remarkable strength to forcibly drag her back to the car. But then what? Doing that would only prove that Aly was right about Amy. That Aly's parents were right about her too. That Amy *was* better.

So she kept walking at a normal pace and followed Aly to the Ferris wheel. She watched while Aly hunted for the control board. This time Aly couldn't find it.

"Aly, let's go," Amy called out.

"I want to go on the Ferris wheel," Aly said stubbornly.

Amy was losing patience. "Well, you can't. I don't care how good you are with your hands, you're not going to make that thing move."

"I'm not giving up," Aly declared. "I don't care if I have to stay here all night!"

"I don't want to stay here all night," Amy objected.

"Then you can go home," Aly said.

"And how am I supposed to get there?" Amy asked.

"How should I know?" Aly shot back. "Walk. Or maybe you can fly. That wouldn't surprise me. You can do everything else."

"Aly!" Amy wailed.

But Aly ignored her and continued to poke around the base of the Ferris wheel. Amy was fed up. This time she couldn't push away the fact that Aly was acting like a big, spoiled baby.

"Well, I'm leaving!" she yelled.

"Goodbye," Aly yelled back.

Still Amy hesitated. She didn't want to leave Aly here alone. But Aly wasn't giving her a choice.

"Goodbye!" Amy shouted. Turning, she began to walk off in the opposite direction. It would be a long walk home, and she'd have a lot of explaining to do to her mother, but there was no way around it.

She kept walking, but not too fast, hoping Aly would call out to her or that she'd hear Aly's footsteps, running to catch up. When she reached the chain-link fence, she couldn't resist turning around, thinking that just maybe Aly had given up and was following her.

But she couldn't see Aly at all. Not until she looked up. Aly was climbing up the metal bars that crisscrossed the Ferris wheel.

"Aly!" Amy screamed. And at full speed, she sprinted back.

fifteen 15

As she ran, Amy kept an eye on the figure climbing the Ferris wheel. Even from this distance, she could see the tension on Aly's face and in her body as Aly tried to hold on to the cables and posts that made up the wheel. She was stretching and straining to reach each level, struggling to maintain her grip.

Why is she doing this? Amy thought wildly. *What is she trying to prove?* Of course, Amy already knew the answer.

She has to show that she's as tough as I am. That she's as strong, as agile, as good as I am. She won't be satisfied until she can be like me.

But Aly could never be like Amy. It just wasn't in her.

Amy saw a tremor go through Aly's body, and she knew Aly was weakening. "Hold on, Aly! Hold on, I'm coming!"

She knew Aly couldn't hear her. But something made Aly look over her shoulder at Amy. Her face reflected exhaustion, fear—and something else. An awful realization that she wasn't going to make it.

Amy went into a flying leap, the kind of jump no normal human would ever be able to do, the kind of move she was never supposed to make when anyone was watching. But she had to get herself as high on that wheel as possible, as fast as possible. She could see the shock on Aly's face—but whether it was the shock of what Aly was seeing or of what she was feeling, Amy couldn't tell. It didn't really matter; it was her reaction that counted. Aly released her grip on the cable she held and began to plummet.

Amy scrambled across the wheel and tried to break her fall. But even with her ability to respond rapidly to situations and her super speed, she couldn't get to the right spot fast enough. Aly hit the ground.

Amy dropped down and ran to the outstretched figure. Aly lay ominously still on her back. But, bending over her, Amy saw the slight rise and fall of her chest. She was still alive.

With phenomenal speed, Amy dashed to the fence, scrambled over it, and ran out into the street. She waved frantically at passing cars, and someone pulled over.

"There's been an accident! Someone fell off the Ferris wheel!"

Thank goodness the woman behind the wheel had a car phone. She immediately dialed 911. Amy ran back to the fence and, with a strength that surprised even her, broke open the padlock on the gate.

It only took a couple of minutes for the ambulance to arrive, but to Amy it felt like hours. Within seconds two paramedics were lifting the unconscious Aly onto a stretcher. Amy climbed into the ambulance behind her.

As the ambulance sped off, one of the men in the back adjusted an oxygen mask over Aly's face. The other had a portable phone in his hand, and he spoke to Amy. "What's your home phone number?"

Amy automatically began to recite her own number, and then she realized that the man was assuming they were twin sisters living in the same home. She told him the Kendrickses' number instead. But as he dialed, she remembered that the Kendrickses weren't home. She listened to him leave a message on the answering machine, telling them that one of their daughters had been in an accident and was being taken to the emergency room at Westside Hospital.

Even with the sirens wailing, Amy could hear Aly's labored breathing. And there was no way she could avoid seeing the blood that traveled down from the wound on Aly's head. "Your sister's going to be okay," a paramedic said. But Amy knew he was just saying that to keep her calm. He couldn't really be sure.

They arrived at the hospital. Amy jumped out and followed the stretcher through the emergency entrance. A nurse took over, giving a quick look at Aly and directing the paramedics. "Examining room three!"

Amy tried to follow them, but the nurse held her back. "I'm sorry, dear, you can't go with her," she said gently.

"But she's my twin!" Amy pleaded.

"I know, I can see that. But you'll have to stay here in the waiting room. I'll come back and tell you what's happening, I promise." She ushered Amy to a seat, then hurried off in the direction where Aly had been taken.

Amy was dimly aware of other people in the room, but she didn't take any notice of them. She could only tremble and think.

Aly had to live, she had to be okay. Or Amy would never forgive herself. Because she knew that this was all her fault. Aly would never have tried anything so foolish if she hadn't been trying to prove something to Amy. None of this would have been happening if Amy hadn't gone to the Hillcrest Recreation Center in search of another Amy.

Suddenly the nurse came running back into the waiting room and beckoned to Amy. "Your sister needs an immediate blood transfusion, and we don't have enough of her type here right now. If we wait for delivery from the blood bank, it could be too late. Will you agree to give her blood?"

"My blood?" Amy asked in a quavering voice.

"Yes, we won't even have to take the time to type it. You're identical twins, you have to be a perfect match."

At that moment the door of the emergency room burst open and Mr. Kendricks ran in. Mrs. Kendricks was close behind. They saw Amy and ran toward her. "Aly!" Mrs. Kendricks shrieked.

"No, I'm Amy!"

"Aly needs blood immediately," the nurse told them. "Do we have your permission to take blood from Aly's twin?"

Amy stood stock-still, a million thoughts racing, crashing, colliding in her head in the space of half a second. Blood, her blood. The blood that would reveal everything. Her unique genetic structure, her DNA, the great secret that she had to keep to herself—the doctors and nurses would know all. And word would leak out that a genetically designed clone had been discovered at

Westside Hospital. Any hope she might have for a semi-normal life would be forever gone. She would become a subject for tests, experiments, research . . . and the organization would find her. Their plans for a master race would become once again a real and horrible possibility. Amy could almost hear the earth quiver. Her blood could change the world—and not for the better.

And then there was Aly, who could die without this blood.

Amy knew what she had to do. She began to roll up her shirtsleeve. "Take my blood," she said.

The nurse hurried her into the examining room, and the Kendrickses followed. Now Mrs. Kendricks wept in relief, and she kept murmuring, "Thank you, Amy, thank you." Still unconscious, Aly lay on a table. Another table was rolled over and placed just next to her.

"We'll do a direct transfusion from Amy to Aly to save time," the nurse said. A pole was placed between the tables, and a plastic bag was hung from it.

Amy climbed onto the empty table and lay down. She could see the Kendrickses. Mrs. Kendricks smiled encouragingly through her tears. Mr. Kendricks looked relieved—no, more than relieved. He almost looked . . . *excited.*

The pungent smell of alcohol tickled Amy's nose as the nurse swabbed a place on her inner arm. She adjusted the plastic bag on the pole and took the tube that hung from it. A needle protruded from the very end of the tube. The nurse tapped Amy's arm to raise a vein and brought the needle closer. . . .

Amy closed her eyes.

There was a rush of air as the door burst open. "Stop!"

Amy opened her eyes. Dr. Hopkins stood there. "Don't transfuse from her!" he yelled.

"But, Doctor, it's an emergency!" the nurse protested.

"What's the patient's blood type?" he demanded.

The nurse told him.

"That's my type too," Dr. Hopkins announced. He pulled Amy off the table and took her place there. The nurse still looked confused, but she followed his directions and swabbed his inner arm.

Amy looked at the Kendrickses. She could still read the relief in their faces. But the excitement she had noticed in Mr. Kendricks's expression was gone.

sixteen

16

It was a variation on an old, familiar dream. There was the row of identical babies, each in her own glass case. The cases were numbered, one through thirteen. But there was something different about the thirteenth. Across the cover of the case, a word had been stamped in red: REJECTED.

And now there were hands opening the case, lifting the baby out of it. Amy cried out. "No, don't take her away, she's one of us."

And a voice from far away answered her. "But she's not an Amy. Not an Amy. Not an Amy . . . Amy . . . *Amy*!"

Amy opened her eyes. She was back in the waiting

room, lying on a sofa. Dr. Hopkins was sitting by her side, and he was smiling.

"Aly's going to be all right," he told her. "She's resting comfortably."

Relief fell over Amy like a blanket, warm and soft and comforting. "Can I see her?"

"Very briefly," Dr. Hopkins said. He helped Amy off the sofa and took her by the hand, as if she was a little girl. For once Amy didn't mind.

Mr. and Mrs. Kendricks were standing by Aly's bed. Aly's eyes were open, but they were cloudy and vague, as if she wasn't completely awake.

"Hi, Aly," Amy said softly. Aly's eyes moved slowly in her direction.

"Amy . . ." Her voice was drowsy.

"Yes, it's me. Dr. Hopkins says you're going to be fine."

"Amy," Aly repeated. "Amy . . . I saw you fly."

"I can't fly, Aly."

"But I saw you . . . you jumped up from the ground, you flew onto the Ferris wheel. . . ."

Dr. Hopkins leaned over and stroked Aly's forehead. "It was just a dream, Aly. Just a dream."

"Okay," Aly murmured, and her eyes closed.

Then Dr. Hopkins motioned to Mr. Kendricks. The plump man nodded, kissed his wife gently on the cheek, and left the room with the doctor and Amy.

"I know who you are now," Dr. Hopkins said to Mr. Kendricks. "I thought you looked familiar the first time I saw you, but I didn't recognize you then. You didn't have the beard twelve years ago, did you?"

"No," Mr. Kendricks said. "And I was about fifty pounds lighter."

Amy looked back and forth between the two men in utter confusion. "What are you talking about?"

"Mr. Kendricks was with Project Crescent," Dr. Hopkins told her.

Amy gasped. "You were a scientist?"

Mr. Kendricks smiled slightly. "No. I was the laboratory janitor and general handyman. I cleaned up, and I fixed things. Electricity, plumbing, locks and keys . . ."

So that was why Aly was so good with her hands, Amy thought. She'd learned from her father.

"How much did you actually know about what we were doing?" Dr. Hopkins asked him.

"I didn't understand the science," Mr. Kendricks admitted. "But I knew you were making babies in there. And not just regular test-tube babies—special ones, and they were all called Amy. I heard you folks talking. These babies, these Amys . . . you were doing something to make them all geniuses, or athletes, or some kind of superheroes. They would grow up to be better than anyone else. Perfect."

It was all starting to make sense to Amy. "How did you get Aly?" she asked.

"Dr. Jaleski, he was the director . . . anyway, he asked me to take Amy, Number Thirteen, to some sort of adoption agency. I was supposed to leave her there."

"But you didn't," Dr. Hopkins said.

"No. You see, my wife and I, we hadn't been able to have children of our own, and we wanted them. We were trying to adopt, but I wasn't making much money back then, and if you couldn't afford a private adoption, you had to wait a long time. We were already older than most people who were trying to adopt kids, and we knew we might never get one. So when I found myself holding this baby who didn't belong to anyone, well . . ."

"You just decided to keep Number Thirteen," Amy said. The way Nancy had decided to keep Number Seven.

"Yeah. My wife didn't want to call her Amy, though. She thought that was too ordinary. No offense," he said quickly to Amy. "Anyway, we never took our names off the adoption lists, and three years later, we got our son. Now we have a real family. I started my own company, we bought a nice home . . . we've been very happy."

"Even though Aly didn't turn out to be a genius or a superhero?" Dr. Hopkins asked.

Aly's father shrugged. "When she grew up normal,

we just figured your experiment had been a flop, but we didn't care. Sure, it would have been nice for her if she'd turned out to be special in some way. Like really smart, or a great athlete. But that didn't matter to us. She was special just the way she was."

"But then you met Amy."

Mr. Kendricks nodded. "We figured out right away that she had to be one of those Project Crescent babies. And when we saw how superior she was . . ." Now he looked embarrassed. "Well, we kind of hoped our Aly could pick up some of that. Just because it would give her some advantages, a better chance to make it in the world, y'know?"

"That's why you were eager that the transfusion be with *my* blood!" Amy exclaimed.

"Right. I thought if Aly got a drop of your blood in her, she'd get some of your genes."

"It wouldn't have worked," Dr. Hopkins told him. "A drop of blood, even a blood transfusion, wouldn't change Aly's genetic structure."

"Yeah, I kind of suspected that," Mr. Kendricks said. He turned to Amy. "I'm sorry, honey. We weren't trying to take anything away from you, really. We just wanted the best for our daughter."

"It's okay," Amy said. "I understand."

Mr. Kendricks glanced back at the door leading to

Aly's room. "Now all I want is for our little girl to make a full recovery and be her normal, ordinary self again."

"She will," Dr. Hopkins assured him.

Tears filled Aly's father's eyes. "We always thought she was perfect, you know. Just the way she is."

"Maybe you could tell her that once in a while," Amy said.

Mr. Kendricks nodded. Then he turned away and disappeared back into the hospital room.

Amy gazed at the calendar on the kitchen wall. "Aly must be home from the hospital by now."

Her mother came up behind her and put an arm around her. "Yes, I think so."

"But I shouldn't call her, should I." It was a statement, not a question, because Amy already knew the answer.

"No, honey, you shouldn't. You understand why, don't you?"

Amy nodded. She knew that her mother had had some long talks with the Kendrickses, and all the parents were in agreement. It wasn't good for the girls to get together, to have any contact with each other. Because Aly would always try to be like Amy, and she would hurt herself trying.

"What are they going to tell Aly when she wants to call me?"

Her mother's voice was unusually gentle. "They're going to tell her that she's not allowed to see you anymore. That you're a troublemaker and a bad influence on her. That you were never a real friend."

Amy flinched. It was awful, thinking that Aly might really be convinced of that.

"The Kendricks family is moving to the East Coast," Nancy continued. "Mr. Kendricks is expanding his business, and they're going to start a new life out there."

"But they're really doing that just to keep Aly away from me?"

"It hurts, I realize that, Amy. But it's for Aly's own good." Her mother hugged her. "Yours too."

"I know," Amy said sadly. She let out a sigh, and to her own ears, it almost had the sound of a small sob. "Well, at least maybe she won't have to take figure skating anymore." She took a deep breath. "I think I'll go for a walk." She was halfway to the door when she paused and looked back at her mother.

"Mom . . . I don't want to take piano lessons anymore."

Her mother smiled. "Okay."

Outside, Amy couldn't decide which way to walk, and she didn't feel much like walking anyway. So when

Tasha opened her front door and beckoned to her, she went over.

"Want to hang out?" Tasha asked.

"Yeah, okay." But Amy paused at Tasha's door. "Dwayne's not here, is he?"

"No. That's all over."

"Oh. Are you okay about it?"

Tasha nodded. "It's kind of a relief, actually. I got tired of playing dumb all the time. How's Aly?" she asked as Amy walked into the house.

"She's home from the hospital. But I won't be seeing her anymore. They're moving away."

"Oh."

"It's just as well," Amy said. "I think I was getting a little tired of playing wild and crazy party animal. Is Eric home?"

"No, he went over to Lauren's. He got his Spanish assignment back today, and he wanted to show it to her."

"How did he do?"

"He got an A. Can you believe it?"

"That's great," Amy said mournfully. He had to be really grateful to Lauren for this. He probably worshipped the ground she walked on now, considering what she'd done for him. They'd be inseparable.

The girls settled down in the living room. "Dwayne left that mummy video here. Want to watch it?"

Amy wrinkled her nose. "Got anything else?"

"*Grease.*"

"Perfect."

John Travolta and Olivia Newton-John were just telling each other "You're the one that I want" when Eric walked in. "Hi," he said, slumping down on the sofa.

"Hi," Amy replied. "Congratulations, I heard about the A."

"Yeah, pretty cool, huh?" He was looking very pleased with himself.

"Lauren must have been happy," Amy added.

"No kidding. I had to pay her more than she would have gotten if I'd only made a B. That A cost me fifty bucks."

Amy blinked. "You paid her *fifty dollars*?"

"Yeah, that's what she charges for tutoring. She wasn't going to give me a discount—it's not like we were friends or anything."

A good chunk of Amy's depression was lifted from her shoulders. "Hey, you guys want to go to the movies tonight?" she asked hopefully.

"I can't," Eric said. "I don't have any money left. Not a dime." He sounded aggrieved. "You know, Amy, if you'd been willing to help me with Spanish for free, I could have treated both of us to a movie. Plus a giant popcorn. Maybe even a pizza after."

Amy smiled. "How about if I treat tonight?"

It was a nice evening, and it distracted her from the events of the past few days. But when she got home and checked her e-mail, she recognized a sender's name. She opened the mail.

Amy, my parents say I can't see you anymore, and we're moving to Maine. But we can still stay friends. We can keep in touch by e-mail, and they won't ever know. Okay? Write me back right away.

Amy read the message twice and became aware of a burning sensation behind her eyes. Then her vision seemed to blur.

But she could still see well enough to move the cursor in the right direction. And click on "delete."